IMPOSSIBLE LOVE

Charlotte White

A Judy Sullivan Book
Walker and Company
New York

First published in the United States of America
in 1984 by the Walker Publishing Company, Inc.

Published simultaneously in Canada by John Wiley & Sons
Canada, Limited, Rexdale, Ontario.

Library of Congress Cataloging in Publication Data

White, Charlotte, 1944—
    Impossible love.

    "A Judy Sullivan book."
    I. Title.
PS3573.H457214   1984   813'.54   83.-40432
ISBN 0-8027-0777-7

Printed in the United States of America

10 9 8 7 6 5 4 3 2 1

Chapter One

LYNN MARSH SAUNTERED through her own private section of the heavily wooded Missouri Ozarks. Summer was at its prime. Everything she saw was lush and lovely, and the unique beauty of the forest assailed her other senses as well. Layers of leaves and pine needles cushioned her steps, and the scent of evergreens and rich, pungent earth filled her with quiet delight. And as for the woodland sounds, well . . . they were of an unparalleled musical cadence. Even though this area was familiar to her by now, its sensual richness was a constant source of enchantment.

Paddy, Lynn's enthusiastic little beagle, was supposed to be walking with her. Instead, he was scampering hither and yon, yipping joyously at every rabbit and squirrel he encountered.

"Silly old dog," she told him, "how can we have a quiet, peaceful walk to observe nature if you're going to make such a racket?"

The dog looked back at her with a foolish grin, as if to let her know he realized she didn't mean a word of it, that she would have left him back at the cabin if she really wanted to see small animals and birds at close range. To prove his point, he gave a high-pitched yelp and went bounding across the woods in pursuit of a squirrel he didn't stand a chance of catching. Despite his rambunctiousness, Paddy was a friendly dog who had never harmed another living creature. Some watchdog, she mused, for a woman alone in a rather remote area. Paddy might give the warning, but if real danger approached, Lynn suspected he'd be found under a bed or in some other safe haven.

A gentle wind stirred and Lynn paused to breathe deeply. With one hand, she lifted her thick, dark hair so that the breeze could touch against the dampness that had formed at the back of her neck. In the beginning, this life had been a retreat, an escape. Now it was what she wanted. Here she had found peace, a sense of inner and outer serenity that hadn't existed in St. Louis—or in any of the other places she had ever been. Sometimes, of course, she got a bit lonely, but she had learned long ago that loneliness was preferable to pain and deceit.

Lynn wasn't a hermit, yet she could understand what Thoreau had found at Walden. This was her piece of earth, her place of sublime anonymity. Today she wasn't lonely. It had been a busy, hectic day in her arts and crafts shop in the nearby town of St. Clair. From early morning till well past six o'clock, every moment had been occupied. She had been besieged by a constant flow of activity: customers crowding around the cash register to pay and ask questions, artists trying to sell her their wares, the phone ringing off the wall. Tomorrow she would be ready for it again. This evening, however, she was thoroughly enjoying the respite from human voices. If she wanted to talk to Paddy, she could. If she didn't, he wouldn't mind. And above all, he wouldn't talk back except, of course, with a happy bark and a wagging tail.

> "O Shenandoah, I love your daughter
> Away, you rolling river
> For her I've crossed the rolling water,
> Away, we're bound away,
> Across the wide Missouri."

At the sound of the male voice, Lynn froze. She had thought she was alone, that there was no one around for miles. Now someone was shattering the silence with his discordant song. Whoever he was, she thought, he'd never make a living as a singer. If the words hadn't been familiar to her, she would never have recognized the song from its tune. She was reasonably sure "Shenandoah" had not ever been rendered in quite that fashion before.

Hearing the strange voice also, Paddy jerked up his ears and stuck his tail stiffly out. "Shhh, Paddy," she whispered, "don't bark."

For once in his unruly life, the beagle obeyed and followed quietly at her heels as she walked across the bed of springy pine needles. Stepping from the covering foiliage into a clearing, she looked out at the river that crossed her land, then meandered through the valley and flowed far beyond. Someday she meant to follow the river, see where it led, learn where it ended or find out if it just flowed on forever. Several varieties of fish lived in the river. Lynn didn't try to catch them. Often she would just sit on the bank and watch them skim beneath the surface. Occasionally one would get especially brave and make a graceful, arching leap against the skyline.

Anger seized her when she saw the unmelodious singer. Outfitted in plaid shirt and rubber hip boots, he was standing knee deep in *her* river. At every boundary point, she had placed signs that clearly stated: PRIVATE PROPERTY. NO HUNTING OR FISHING ALLOWED. In blatant disregard of those postings, this loud stranger had crossed onto her land to fish from her section of the river. Although she would have thought his singing would scare anything away, it was apparent he was having success. The cooler by his side contained several fish. She wondered how many of them had been caught on her property.

As she passed into the open, her right foot broke a dry stick in two with a rather forceful cracking sound. The fisherman had just gotten to "O Shenandoah, I'll not deceive you" when the noise made him stop and turn around. His eyes widened in surprise at the sight of the young woman and the dog standing there. Recovering quickly, he gave a big grin and came wading out of the water toward her.

"H'lo there," he called when he was still several yards away. "Where did you come from?"

Lynn didn't reply. She waited until he was much closer, until she could see his keen gray eyes and nearly black hair. Even at first glance, she could tell he was a confident, presumptuous sort. Such tall, good-looking men usually were, and this one had the manner of the wealthy about him. It always showed. Even in the universal garb of jeans and sport shirt, she could spot the to-the-manner-born air.

Propping his rod and reel against a tree, he gave her an assessing look that didn't miss a thing from her neatly parted lustrous hair to the tanned legs extending from the old khaki shorts. Displaying his grin again, he said, "Don't tell me. I can guess. You're a wood sprite or nymph, and they don't talk."

It wasn't easy to contain her anger, but she believed scathing sarcasm would be more effective on this interloper than hot words spilled out of control. In fact, she felt that a display of temper would probably only amuse him. Quite icily, she replied, "Oh, I talk all right. In fact, I was just getting ready to ask you the same question you asked me: where did you come from?"

"Actually, it only seems fair that *you* should answer first since *my* question came before yours."

"Fair?" She uttered the one-word question with an arching of her eyebrows. "That scarcely seems pertinent. After all, I'm where I belong, and I don't really think you can make the same statement."

His brow knitted in puzzlement and he glanced down at Paddy, who was circling frantically around her ankles. He gave a shrug with shoulders so broad they pulled his shirt taut, posing a threat to its seams.

"Uh, I'm Dan Ross. My friend Jess Wicklein is letting me use his place for a little vacation. I have his written permission on me somewhere." He began patting about on the fishing vest and digging in his shirt pockets.

"That isn't necessary, Mr. Ross. I have no reason to doubt that Jess let you use his place. He's a very generous man and often has visitors here."

"Then . . .?" His expression and gestures said, So what's your problem, lady? more clearly than the words themselves could have done.

She gave a deep sigh and continued dryly, "Jess, as I said, often lets his friends and associates hunt and fish on his land. Up till now, it hasn't been a problem. Apparently the others all had a talent you lack: they could read."

He gaped at her in astonishment. Even the gape didn't make him look unattractive. This was an observation that somehow irritated her.

"I strike you as illiterate?" Quirks played at the corners of his mouth betraying signs of amusement, quirks that could easily turn into a smile calculated to melt the hearts of ladies of all ages.

Instead of answering with words, Lynn turned her head with slow deliberation until her line of vision led directly to a white sign posted on a tree.

Dan Ross followed her gaze, then he grew very still and a dark flush spread over his neck and face. Well, at least he has the decency to be embarrassed, she thought. If he had been chagrined, however, he recovered quickly. In place of the apology she had expected, he threw back his head and laughed heartily.

Fury no longer so easily contained took hold of her. "You find it funny, Mr. Ross? Perhaps you'll find it less so when I notify the authorities. I don't know what it's like where you're from, but around here trespassing is illegal."

Evidently seeing the fire in her eye, he stepped slightly backward. "Listen, call the authorities if you want to be that way. I was just out following the river along, happily catching fish, and didn't even notice I had crossed Jess's property line. Whatever you think should be done about this dastardly crime, then by all means do it." She noticed that humor no longer played at his mouth. In fact, it had become a rather grim line that would have been forbidding if she hadn't been so angry. And so *right*. He had no business being here, no matter how innocent he tried to make it sound.

She gave a shrug of her own. Two could play his game. "I'll let it go this time—"

"Big of you," he said sarcastically before she could complete her comment. "Don't do me any favors. If it'll make you happier, I'll go to court, pay a fine, spend a little time in the local slammer. I'd throw back the fish I caught here, but they seem to be dead. Perhaps it would make you happy if I paid for them. Name your price."

He took a wallet out of his pocket, all the while glaring at her. She walked closer to the river and looked out at the rippling expanse of water. Okay, she thought, trying to calm herself down. She was beginning to realize she had overreacted to the situation. It was, admittedly, quite possible to miss the signs if you were following the river.

"Put your money away, Mr. Ross. I suppose I was annoyed that I had been robbed of my solitude. And that can't be restored with cash. Just take your fish and go."

"So sorry. And please be assured I won't be bothering your solitude again. I'll be here several days but will endeavor, in the future, to keep my eyes peeled for your signs."

"That would be appreciated," she said crisply. "Enjoy the rest of your stay." She didn't turn to look at him and was surprised when his hearty laughter rang out again. From where she stood at the river's edge, she twisted around to meet his eyes. "I said something funny?"

"Depends on what type sense of humor you have. If you have one at all. Here I'd always heard what neighborly types resided in the Ozarks and, in addition, Jess had told me what a nice lady lived nearby. You *are* Lynn Marsh?"

She nodded slightly, still mystified by his laughter.

"Anyway," he continued, "you come at me with all the friendliness of a rabid porcupine, then tell me to enjoy the rest of my stay in much the same tone you'd tell me to go to hell."

Irrationally, she saw red. Whether he saw the logic or not, this was her property, her sanctuary. There was no reason why he should be so condescendingly sardonic. She was just on the verge of telling him, in no uncertain terms, to go to hell, when she tripped on a stone, twisted her ankle, and fell into the river.

When his laughter hit her ears again, she lost control completely. With easy swiftness, he had moved toward her to offer assistance. Well, she didn't need his help. She didn't need anyone's help. Struggling to her feet, she stood before him, dripping with anger as well as fresh spring water. Her brown eyes, which in good humor held tiny golden sparkles, had gone totally dark. When he placed supporting hands on her shoulders, she shrugged them off angrily.

"I *am* sorry," he said, although laughter still lit his eyes and caused the crinkles at their corners to deepen. "I know it isn't polite at all to laugh, but . . ."

Lynn looked down at her sodden shoes and socks that were being dampened even more by the water pouring from the hem of her shorts. She felt relief for a moment because no serious damage had been done to her foot. Paddy, safely dry, was running around in excitement. From time to time, he eyed the fisherman tentatively as if trying to decide if he should be friendly or not. Then suddenly, for no accountable reason, her mood did a turnabout.

"Okay," she said, responding to Dan Ross's infectious grin with a smile of her own—a slightly embarrassed smile. "I'm ready to call a halt to this spontaneous mountain feud. It's obvious that I shan't win in any event. How can I hope to put up a good fight when I can't even stand on my own two feet?"

"Then I'm forgiven for laughing at your predicament?"

She took a step forward, shaking her head at the squishing sound her shoes made. "I guess I'll have to forgive you. Not even I am hardheaded enough to try to blame you for my dunking. It was due to a sorry combination of fury and clumsiness. And I'm also willing to admit it must have a funny side. From a spectator's point of few, that is. From my point of view, it's wet."

9

Moving back toward the edge of the wooded area, she sat down on a bed of pine needles and began to remove her wet sneakers and terry socks.

He looked down at her with mock solemnity. "I suppose it would be too much to ask to be forgiven for the trespassing also?"

"I'll think about it," she said lightly.

"Then I'll sit with you while you give the matter careful consideration." Long legs stretched before him, he sat down beside her at the edge of the forest. By this time, Paddy had decided to be friendly and jumped all over Dan, nudging him, licking him, and tramping him with his paws.

"Paddy, settle down," Lynn said.

"That's all right. I like dogs," Dan replied. Paddy did, however, grow a bit calmer as Dan patted his sleek head and chubby little body.

Lynn watched the man and the dog for a moment, then looked out at the river, which was picking up different hues from the rays of a sun that would be setting before long. When she thought about her behavior, she was somewhat appalled. Perhaps she was getting too much like a hermit. This evening she had certainly exhibited antisocial behavior. Sure, Dan Ross was trespassing, but she could have approached him in a civil manner, saving all the sarcasm and anger until she saw if he deserved it or not. When she looked back at him, a slight flush showed beneath the golden tan color of her cheeks.

"I suppose," she said softly, "that I should be the one asking forgiveness. I don't know what came over me. I'd tell you I had a hard day at work—which I did—but that's no excuse for pouncing on you like a veritable harridan."

"I did trespass."

"True, but I didn't have to react like someone from the Hatfield or McCoy clan. Maybe, and it's no real excuse, I was startled as much as annoyed. I'm so used to not having anyone at all around and was merely rambling around soaking up nature. Then I heard you singing and standing there, bigger than life, right in the middle of *my* river.'' At her own words, she smiled ruefully. That was another indication of how ingrown and possessive she had become. Was it really possible to own a river?

"Have you always lived around here, Lynn?''

Looking down at the earth, she shook her head. "Only a few years. I run a small arts and crafts shop in St. Clair. Before that, I was city born and bred.''

She carefully did not say which city. When talking to other people, Lynn gave away as few details about herself and her past as she could. Both FBI agents and underworld figures had been very clever with ruses in the past to obtain information. For all she knew, this man could belong to either side. If she had learned anything at all during the last few years, it was that she couldn't tell the difference. Smooth-talking, "sincere'' people represented both factions.

"I think I would have guessed that anyway,'' he said with a small laugh. "You don't quite have enough twang in your voice to be a native.''

"I'm working on it. Where are you from?''

"Illinois. I'm what you call 'city born and bred,' too. Actually, this is one of my first ventures with the hunting and fishing bit. Which also provides me with a good excuse for not checking out the boundaries and signs more closely. In truth, it probably isn't even safe for me to be out alone like this. At least I opted for the fishing rod over the rifle or shotgun. This way I'm not endangering anyone. Not even myself.''

"I don't know if it was a wise choice or not,'' she said wryly. "If you'd been carrying a loaded weapon, I might have thought twice about attacking you verbally.''

"It's a thought,'' he replied with an easy grin, "but I'm such a novice I probably would have shot my own foot instead of you anyway.''

She aimed a look toward the container of fish. "Novice? It seems to me that you've made quite a haul.''

"Beginner's luck.''

"Well,'' she said, standing up slowly, "I'd better get on

back. Again, Mr. Ross, I'm sorry for my rudeness. It embarrasses me."

"And I'm sorry for my trespassing. And for my bad singing which you were unlucky enough to overhear. Also, I'm still sorry I laughed when you got wet."

"That makes us an awfully sorry pair. Perhaps we should quit apologizing before it gets out of hand."

"Join me for dinner tonight? I'll fry the fish. Nice of me, isn't it, to offer you your own fish?"

"Thanks for the offer," she said gently but firmly, "but I've already eaten. Enjoy your vacation, Mr. Ross."

"Dan," he prompted.

"All right, Dan. Good evening."

She walked several steps away from him. Without looking back, she knew he was watching her.

"Lynn?" he called.

Turning her head only, she looked back. "Yes?"

"If I put the fish on ice till tomorrow night, will you accept my invitation?"

She swallowed hard, not wanting to seem any ruder than she had already been. There was no way she could accept his invitation. He could be anybody. Even leaving the drama of her colorful past out of the situation, he could be married. And even if he were innocuous and single, she still couldn't risk much in the way of friendship or social activity. People asked questions, and too many of her answers to standard questions were, by necessity, evasive.

"I can't, Dan. I really can't. But it has nothing to do with hard feelings. Now, good evening."

Before he could pursue the matter, she ran into the covering woods, legs moving as swiftly as a young deer's, and Paddy ran with her, going twice as far as she did because of all the extra circles he made in his never-ending game of chase.

Back at the cabin, Lynn slipped off her wet clothes, bathed, and put on her softly woven nightshirt. It was early to prepare for bed, with night not completely fallen, but she was too tired to dress again, and there was no one to see or care. She sat curled up in an easy chair by the open window and tried to read, but she could not concentrate on the printed words. Giving up, she just watched the night grow darker and darker, the colors of the setting sun showing through the tree branches, fading gradually until there was no light left at all. The moon was only a pale sliver and the sky was black and starless.

The events of the evening had unsettled her. She couldn't pretend to herself that they hadn't. What was going to become of her? Earlier in the day she had congratulated herself on the peace she had found, on the completeness of her life. Now she saw things from a very different perspective. Perhaps all she had really found was escape from life itself.

She was twenty-five years old and she had no lover, no husband, no child. Her parents were both dead and she had no brothers or sisters. She knew everyone in St. Clair and they all knew her, yet she had no close friends. Once she had hoped for so much more. She had wanted to be an actress or a model. She had wanted to marry a handsome, laughing man and have a whole houseful of beautiful, laughing children. Those things were as far out of reach for her now as the sun, the moon, and the stars.

Lynn Marsh. That wasn't even her name. Oh, it was now. She and her mother had had an attorney they knew well quietly, and rather expensively, make the name changes legal. Linda and Claire Marshall no longer existed. After enough papers were signed, all the birth certificates, drivers' licenses, social security cards, passports—everything—had carried the names Lynn and Evelyn Marsh. They had even been afraid to use her mother's maiden name, and Claire Haynes Marshall had been buried in a grave in a small country cemetery near St. Clair with a headstone that said Evelyn Elizabeth Marsh.

She had died too young. Most of her adult life, she had suffered from a mild form of hypertension, but the stress and strain had caused the disease to go out of control. Perhaps, Lynn mused unhappily, her mother had been lucky that the stroke had been fatal instead of leaving her paralyzed or otherwise seriously impaired.

Davy Marshall. Lord, how they had loved that man. He had treated them as if they were a queen and princess, and to them he had certainly been a king. He had been an attractive, though slightly fleshy, man with an easygoing, charismatic charm Everyone liked Davy Marshall. His was a typical rags-to-riches story: a poor kid from a bad section of St. Louis who managed to put himself through college and go on to become an entrepreneur—a sort of corporate whiz who had only to touch a business venture to have it become a success.

From what Lynn knew of the situation, he had been wealthy and well-established before he met and married Claire, a blonde beauty almost young enough to be his daughter. He had wanted children—lots of them, especially sons to inherit his empire—but Claire, after producing Linda, had a series of miscarriages followed by a hysterectomy. His paternal dotings, then, were focused on Linda. And truly, he had treated Claire more like a child than a wife.

They had accepted what he told them without question. What reason had they to doubt? They had the lavish apartment in the city, the spacious home in the country, the cabin in the Ozarks, luxury automobiles, designer clothes, vacations at any time and place they wished. Davy's corporations and business ventures were too numerous for his family to even know the names of them all.

"Don't bother your pretty little head with it," he had always laughed when Linda asked questions. "You'll never have to work a day in your life, princess. Daddy's seen to that."

Any curiosity she felt was assuaged when he dangled a new bauble in front of her. She felt dumb now at not having suspected anything, but, after all, she had only been seventeen when her world fell apart around her. And her mother hadn't been a stupid woman either, only a naive one who wasn't experienced in the ways of the world and who regarded her husband with complete love and trust.

Lynn didn't believe the memory of that awful day would ever fade. Eight years hadn't diminished it. There were nights she still woke up in a cold sweat, and the flashes from the cameras seemed to be blinding her eyes. "How do you feel about your father's arrest, Miss Marshall?" "When did you first learn he was connected with the Afton bombings, Miss Marshall?" She had stood on the steps of the exclusive girls' school, too terrified to run, too terrified to speak. Later, she had learned that another set of reporters had descended upon her mother in the same fashion at their home in Frontenac.

What a way to learn. They hadn't wanted to believe it. They tried very hard not to believe it. When the newspapers reported the evidence against him, Claire and Linda learned about it for the first time. Not once did either of them ask him if he were innocent or guilty. His eyes told the truth when he looked at them, and they didn't want to hear him lie. During the visits at the jail, they talked of weather, the horses, baseball—of everything except what mattered.

Someone from a rival gang managed to get at Davy Marshall with a gun, and he was permanently silenced before the trial. Or perhaps the gunman hadn't been from a rival gang, but from Davy's own—sent by those who were afraid he would name names to save his own skin to some extent.

Thinking back on it, Lynn felt hard and cold. All the tears had been shed a long time ago, and none were left. The proof was irrefutable. Linda had heard of the New York Mafia, Chicago gangsters, Detroit street warfare. She had read the St. Louis daily papers enough to know her own hometown wasn't exactly corruption-free, but that had nothing to do with her clean, shining world. Hah. Davy Marshall hadn't just been a part of one of the biggest crime rings in St. Louis—he was the head of it. Every racket that existed had Marshall and his gang lurking in the background somewhere.

Oh, some of the businesses had been legitimate. These were the ones Claire had sold at bargain prices. All that was dirty and soiled, she walked off and left. That included the near-mansion in Frontenac. She had invested the money carefully so that the interest income was enough to support her and her daughter. Their life-style hadn't exactly been extravagant after that, but both had developed a bitterness toward lavishness. All they had wanted was peace and simplicity, and that hadn't been easily obtained.

No one had ever quite believed that Davy Marshall's wife and daughter were as innocent as they claimed. They were hounded and questioned constantly by both the FBI and gangsters. A lot of cash and jewels had never surfaced after Davy's arrest. Maybe they would have cracked him. Maybe not. He died before they had a chance to find out.

It had been a nightmare. Linda had been asked to leave the exclusive school. No reason was given, and she didn't ask for one. Claire's "friends" dropped her quickly. All the marvelous clubs and societies to which she belonged no longer wanted her as a member. Charities didn't even want her volunteer work anymore. Claire and Linda were threatened and warned. The police and FBI agents weren't a lot kinder than the various gang members, although Lynn assumed it had been a gang member who had wired her mother's empty car to explode.

"Next time you could be in a car like that. Think about it."

That's what the note had said. They thought about it. That's when they changed their names, left for Paris, and stayed for four years. Four years was enough. They were hungry for America. Using a large portion of their principal, they bought the acreage and a cabin in the Ozarks. Lynn had never been sure what happened to the other property they had owned there. She really didn't care. Undoubtedly it had been purchased with blood money, and she wanted no part of it. Together she and her mother had started The Calico Cat, selling wicker baskets, handmade quilts, and walnut bowls, gradually adding to their stock until they had the best selection of handcrafted objects in the area. Two years ago her mother had died. Since then, Lynn had been alone.

As she had told herself earlier, it wasn't a bad life, and there were worse things than being alone. She preferred the solitude to constant harassment and a never-ending stream of questions she could not answer.

But she didn't want to become withdrawn and hostile, an alien to life and laughter. This evening had shown her she was certainly headed in that direction.

How wonderful it would have been, she thought, to be able to walk up to the fisherman and laughingly pass the time of day, agree to a dinner date, or at least spend some time pleasantly and companionably. And maybe they would even fall in love.

But that was out of the question. She simply couldn't risk losing the privacy it had taken her so long to gain, so revealing her true identity was impossible. And Lynn also knew from experience that no man would ever want to become seriously involved with Davy Marshall's little girl—not even eight long years after his death. The reasons were crystal clear why Lynn Marsh must never permit herself to fall in love.

Chapter Two

AFTER ONLY AN hour or so at the shop the next morning, Lynn became resigned to another busy day. The tourist season was at its peak, and it seemed that lady campers had to relieve their rustic living with a good deal of shopping. And, although she grew tired, she wasn't complaining. During the long, cold winter months, her customers were few and far between. In the winter, she ran The Calico Cat with only occasional part-time help. In the summer, she hired high school and college kids to work full-time.

The past few days had been so busy that Lynn wondered if her two girls, Julie and Kim, were enough. One of the biggest problems was children. Their mothers would become so engrossed in the needlework and decorated butter churns that they didn't watch them. Most were okay, but a few who were especially unruly had been known to break delicate items. Often the damage wouldn't be noticed until the culprit was long gone, such as when a shelf was rearranged or dusted and an arm or leg would fall off a china doll as soon as it was touched.

Trying to keep an eye on a pair of impish preschoolers at the same time she carefully packaged some hand-blown glassware for a customer, Lynn reached up to push away a tendril of hair that had fallen across her forehead. A fat lady in a loudly printed blouse and a funny hat was waddling toward her, carrying a metal milk can.

"Isn't this a bit high for a milk can?" she asked truculently. "I was raised on a farm and I know what milk cans cost."

Doing her best to smile graciously, Lynn explained, "The price really isn't for the milk can itself. It's for the artwork on the side. Dawn Jarrel's work is in great demand now. The Smithsonian Institution has actually contracted for a lot of her work. You'll find cans similar to that offered in their catalog. And at an even higher price. Because she's from this area, she gives us a special rate."

"Well, I don't know," the woman whined. "It seems awfully high to me still."

Lynn kept smiling so hard her gums were beginning to ache. "If you were just wanting milk cans for antique items or to decorate yourself, you might try down the street. There's a very nice antique shop on the corner."

"Pardon me, ma'am, but could I see that can a moment? If you don't mind, of course."

Lynn held her breath in surprise. She would have known that voice anywhere, but she couldn't imagine how he had managed to get inside the shop without her noticing. The obese tourist cast a suspicious look toward Dan Ross. "I suppose you can *look*," she finally said, "but I haven't decided yet."

"Oh, yes, of course," he said quickly. "I realize that you found it before I did. I just wanted a closer look, since it might be the last chance I get."

The woman reluctantly relinquished the metal can to Dan's hands. He turned it around and around with reverence. "A Dawn Jarrel," he said in a voice filled with awe. "I'd know her work anywhere. Look at that exquisite detail. The vining motif and little flowers and that prancing white unicorn. I think it's her unicorns that have done the most to make her famous, don't you, Ms. Marsh?"

"Undoubtedly," Lynn said wryly. If she were a betting woman, she'd lay odds that Dan Ross had never heard of Dawn Jarrel until he walked through the door of her shop and overheard the conversation.

The tourist stood back and regarded the large object in Dan's possession. She narrowed her eyes, tightened her mouth, and began digging about in her huge canvas tote. "Will you take traveler's checks?"

"Sure," Lynn replied smoothly. "Are you sure you really want this item? I don't want you to buy something you'll regret." Lynn could almost see the wheels tuning in the woman's mind, and she knew she had made a sale. Trying to dissuade her had been exactly the right tactic, for it was clear she now thought Lynn wanted to sell the milk can to Dan Ross. And Dan Ross had, she was fairly certain, no desire to buy a milk can —no matter what it had painted on its side.

"I'm sure," the woman stated, tearing out several of the checks and signing them with determination. Giving a coy smile, she continued, "I really intended to buy it all along. I just wanted to see if you'd come down on the price a little. Can't blame a girl for trying, can you?"

"Not at all. Trying never hurts, though the prices here are firm." After she had given the woman her change, she turned the milk can over to Kim to pack. "Enjoy your Dawn Jarrel original. You'll be the envy of all your friends."

While she waited on a few more in line, Dan Ross roamed about the shop, looking everything over carefully. When the pace died down and the woman with the milk can was gone, Lynn looked across the shop to find him grinning at her. She left the counter and walked over to where he stood. "I don't know if I should thank you or not."

"By all means, you should thank me. I helped you unload an overpriced piece of junk."

She shook her head in mock dismay. "Then it's as I thought; you haven't heard of Jarrel."

"I hate to confess my ignorance but a fact is a fact."

"And what I told my customer is a fact, too. Dawn Jarrel does sell to the Smithsonian. As well as prestigious shops in major cities."

"Come on," he said, playfully taunting her, "I made my

confession. You might as well make yours. Did you or did you not make a tidy profit on that item?''

He was an impossible man. He could say the most presumptuous things in a way that made her smile. "Okay," she confided in a stage whisper, "I did. But I told the customer the truth and still pocketed a nice profit. Isn't that what running a business is all about?''

"That's what they tell me. But if I had a wife—which I don't, in case you were wondering and were too shy to ask—I'd be very perturbed it she brought home a milk can with *that* price tag, no matter who put what on its dented little sides."

"But this wife you don't have could be right," she argued playfully. "In my opinion, a Jarrel is a good investment. Our suspicious lady can probably sell that can a year or so from now for twice what she paid me. Talk about a tidy profit."

"Keep talking, lady, and I may buy one yet. Even though I've already done you one favor today. In compensation for my past transgressions."

"I thought we had agreed to forgive and forget on the mutual transgressions."

"That's true. But I have a competitive nature and am a firm believer in one-upmanship. I came in here with the intention of doing you a favor of some sort so you'd owe me one."

She looked at him warily. Getting rid of Dan Ross might not be easy. Especially when she wasn't sure she really wanted to get rid of him. He was single, attractive, and had a great sense of humor. What woman in her right mind would want to get rid of him?

As if sensing her weakening, he pounced. "I still have those blasted fish and I really haven't the slightest idea how to cook them. If you'd reconsider coming to dinner, perhaps you could give me some pointers."

"You want me to come cook your fish for you?" she asked, her dark eyes dancing with amusement. This man had to be one of a kind.

"Well, I said I needed a favor. Besides, I don't mean that I want you to do the cooking. Just give me instructions. If you'd like, I'll provide satin pillows for you to sit on while I slave over a hot stove."

Lynn looked around nervously to make sure Kim and Julie weren't listening. They seemed much too occupied with customers to be hearing her conversation with Dan.

"Dan, I—"

"Can you give me one good reason to refuse? Don't you believe I'm not married? I suppose you might run into that type a lot, but—"

She held up her hand. "If you say you're not, that's good enough for me. That wasn't the reason for my hesitation. And you're perfectly right: I can't give you a good reason. So that's why I can't accept your invitations. My situation in life is . . . well, it's different and difficult to explain. In fact, I can't explain."

"You're not married?" he asked. "I was sure Jess told me—"

"I'm not. I never have been. And that's about the last question I can answer, so . . ."

He gave her a crooked grin that did something strange to her heart. "You're one mysterious lady. But I'll make a deal with you: come to my fish fry tonight and I'll not ask a single personal question. Fact is, I have a secret or two of my own . . . how's that? I warned you that I was competitive."

"Dan," she began, but his impatient gesture silenced her remaining protest.

"One evening fish fry. No questions on either side. I've never been here before. After this week, I may never be back again. What's the harm? My intentions are perfectly honorable. If you'd like, I'll put that in writing and have it notarized before evening."

She drew a deep breath and shook her head. "Anyone tell you that you'd make a great politician?"

A strange looked passed across his face, then was gone as quickly as it had appeared. "Thought we weren't supposed to ask questions."

"It's hard to have a conversation without them," she said ruefully.

"And therein lies the challenge. Are you game?"

Okay, kid, she told herself, now is the moment of decision. She knew she wanted to spend the evening with him. And she wasn't afraid of him. From hard experience, she had learned a lot about human nature, and, unless her powers of perception had failed considerably, this man was a kind man, a strong and good man. What she had to fear the most was from herself: that she would like being with him too much and want more. But, as he said, he probably would go away soon, never to return. He'd go back to wherever he came from in Illinois and she'd stay here in St. Clair.

"All right," she said softly. "I'll come help with the fish. Some of them are undoubtedly mine anyway."

"Great. Any time you're ready, I'll be there with frying pan and can of grease. And bring Paddy along. He's a fine mutt."

"Now I begin to get the picture. It isn't my company you really want. It's Paddy's."

With the lift of a shoulder and a slightly crooked grin, he told her, "That's the chance you'll have to take, pretty lady. There are just some things in life you can't be absolutely sure about."

A new bevy of customers thronged into the little shop, and the young girls shot looks of appeal at Lynn. "Sorry, but I have to go to work. See you tonight."

"Aren't you going to sell *me* something?" he asked, lifting his eyebrows comically.

"You look around," she said severely, "and if you see anything you want, bring it up to the cash register and one of us will take your money."

"Some sales pitch. It's a wonder you have any business at all with such a casual attitude toward your customers."

"Oh, not *all* my customers," Lynn replied as she walked off to assist some of the new entrants. "It's just that after a while I can tell the browsers from the buyers. Besides, something tells me you got exactly what you came in here for."

His hearty laughter pealed out at her, causing everyone in the shop to turn and look at him. If the attention he drew bothered him, he didn't let it show.

A few minutes later, while she was helping a woman select some pillows and afghans, Lynn saw Dan saunter toward the counter. Julie was at the cash register, and Dan put a hand-tooled Western belt and a turquoise ring on the counter, paid for them in cash, and walked out of The Calico Cat after giving Lynn a triumphant look that plainly said, See, you don't know so much.

The rest of the day flew by. In spite of the fact that she kept extremely busy, Lynn's mind was never far from the approaching evening. It was almost as if she were somebody else, somebody new and different. A man had asked her for a date—of sorts. And she had accepted, saying "See you tonight" just as anyone else might do.

For a few pensive moments, she wondered if her life would ever change. She decided it probably wouldn't. For such a young woman, that might seem a terribly pessimistic and fatalistic attitude, but Lynn chose to think of it as simply practical and accepting. During the time she had spent in Paris, she had met a young American student and dated him several times. Mike had been a nice-looking, pleasant boy, and when he exhibited all the signs and symptoms of being smitten, Lynn had decided to confide in him. He had turned somewhat pale but avowed it made no difference in his feelings toward her. After that, however, their relationship went steadily downhill, and soon he no longer came around or called at all.

Although she was hurt at the time, even though she hadn't actually been in love with Mike, she never did blame him for his attitude. He was very young, and the way she told the story of all the harrassing, threats, and the exploding car, she could see why he would turn pale and become less enchanted with her charms. Any boy would. Any man would. The money and jewels had never been found and, until they were, Lynn would always be prey for suspicious underworld gangsters and the FBI.

When, at last, she locked up The Calico Cat and returned to her cabin, she was experiencing a strange mixture of exhilaration and dread. She felt as keyed up as a twelve-year-old in the throes of her first big crush. And, indeed, she thought with a twinge of bitterness, she was nearly that inexperienced.

She dressed slowly, putting on blue cotton slacks and a white shirt that showed her dark coloring to good advantage. Paddy at her heels, she started walking toward the Wicklein cabin. It was a bigger, more luxurious structure than hers. Lynn's own cabin was really apartment-size, containing four small rooms and a bath. The Wicklein place was actually a three-bedroom house; about the only thing that qualified it as a cabin was the log exterior.

Dan must have been watching for her, for as soon as she was in sight of the cabin, he was on the porch waving and smiling happily. Paddy went bounding toward him with great exuberance, just as if he had known Dan all his life. When Dan began to talk to the dog and pat him, Lynn was glad she had brought the beagle with her. He provided a buffer, a safe subject to talk about, to draw attention away from awkward moments. Despite Dan's avowal not to ask questions, Lynn did anticipate some such moments. Where did you live before you came here? Where were your parents from and what did they do? Where did you go to school? Do you visit home often? *Those* were the type of questions people newly acquainted asked. Without them, what could she and Dan discuss? The butterflies in her stomach made her doubt that she could eat much of the fish.

"Come on in, head chef," he called cheerfully. "Let's get started on this. I'm starved."

"I've never been over here before. This is quite a place," she remarked with a shake of her head when she was inside the shining modern kitchen. "Not exactly roughing it, is it? My cabin doesn't have half these conveniences and gadgets, and I live there all the time."

"Ah, well," Dan said with a philosophical sigh, "those who are rich have. And those who are not do without. But if I help you sell a few more of those crazy milk cans, you might be able to afford a gadget or two." Humming contentedly, he pulled a huge apron from a drawer and put it on. It was the sort of apron designed for backyard barbecues and was well-adorned with corny sayings.

"No big white chef's hat to go with that?" she inquired.

"Couldn't find one. The apron isn't mine. I just found it here. Lends a certain air, don't you think?"

Lynn shook her head. "It's not your style. You're more the dignified type. That only makes you look silly."

"Gee, you sure know how to hurt a guy. Now that you've wounded me to the quick, tell me what to do to the fish."

She looked about the enormous chrome and ceramic kitchen and made a quick decision. "First off," she said firmly, "let's fry it outside. If we have a fish fry in here, you'll be smelling it the rest of your visit."

"*Outside?*"

"They have a pit. All we have to do is build an open fire in it and fry the fish in skillets on the grill. Lead the way. It won't take long."

Actually, by the time they had the fire going satisfactorily and the fish prepared and fried, it was quite late. The sun had gone down almost completely. When Lynn had been certain Dan understood when and how to turn the fish, she went inside and boiled some corn on the cob and tossed a salad. When the food was ready they were both ravenous, and they devoured the meal without much ceremony. Paddy lingered about the table and begged. For his efforts, he was rewarded with bits of fish that Lynn had searched carefully for bones.

During a quiet moment, when all three were too full for comfort, Lynn looked across the table at Dan Ross. His eyes caught and held her. Swallowing hard, she looked quickly away and was surprised to note that this was the first moment approaching awkwardness. Preparing the meal and making silly jokes about it had kept them fully occupied until now. The deepest question asked had been, "Do you know where that pepper shaker went?"

Dan cleared the mess away and put the dishes in the washer. "Let's go sit on the deck awhile," he suggested.

The air had cooled considerably and the evening breeze contained a certain dampness. "I think it might rain later tonight."

"I think so, too," she replied, watching a distant streak of lightning zigzag across the sky.

"When I have time to read for pleasure, I like detective novels and mysteries more than anything else. Chandler. Hammett. Shannon."

She glanced at him curiously, caught the drift of his game, and played along. "I enjoy a good mystery, too. But don't leave out the ladies: Christie. Marsh. James. I don't keep up with the modern poets but still occasionally enjoy the old traditional ones. Especially the ululative beauty of Poe's things. Such purity and loveliness despite the macabre subject matter."

She could feel his smile in the darkness more than she could actually see it.

With slow deliberation, he replied, "I don't know if Poe would appreciate being called traditional or not. But I know what you mean. I've always been a sucker for alliteration myself. And the storytelling ballads. 'The Highwayman' is my favorite of those, I think."

"The highwayman came riding, riding, riding up to the old inn door."

"Where Bess, the landlord's daughter, the landlord's black-eyed daughter, sat tying a dark red love knot into her long black hair."

"More or less," he said with a laugh. "Although I'm not sure what a dark red love knot is."

"Neither am I, though I am fairly certain I've never tied one into my hair."

"I play a lot of tennis and racquetball. Only a little golf. My football is limited to an occasional game of touch with friends and young relatives in the backyard. Most of the season, I can take it or leave it, but I get more excited up around the playoffs for the Super Bowl."

I'm not too 'sporty.' I guess it's just laziness. I do plenty of walking and jogging. Beyond that, I'm a washout. Can't even ride a bicycle."

"I've never met anyone who couldn't ride a bicycle before."

"From what I hear, I'm a rarity. Silly things never seemed to want to stand up when I was on them."

"You're supposed to balance it, hold it up yourself."

"I know what I'm supposed to do. It just doesn't work out that way."

Slowly, gently, the game took off, then gathered speed. Against her own will, because she was having a good time, Lynn felt sleepiness overtake her, and she wasn't able to suppress her yawns. "I'd better leave," she said reluctantly. "This has been fun, but I have to go to work again in the morning, not being on vacation like some fortunate people."

"If you have to go, I'll walk you home."

"That isn't necessary. I have Paddy for protection."

Dan looked down fondly at the fat beagle curled up near the deck railing. "Friend, yes. Protection, I'm not so sure. But I'd feel better if I saw you safely home. I hope you won't smack me and call me a chauvinist for that."

Lynn laughed and shook her head emphatically. "I still appreciate a bit of chivalry. Let's walk then, Daniel."

Once out of the clearing, she shivered slightly and was grateful for the height and bulk of Dan Ross. She had never roamed the woods at night. Doing so had a frightening aspect, even with the glow of Dan's flashlight.

After they were well on their way, he remarked, "I told you

we could pass an evening without questions. It wasn't so hard.''

"No," she admitted. "It was fun because it was a novelty, a new game. But it wouldn't work on a regular basis. Humans are simply too curious by nature for that.''

She knew that to be true because she was already deeply curious about what Dan had meant when he had said he had a secret or two himself. And if she felt that sort of curiosity about him, what must he feel toward a woman who had stated she had no intentions of talking about herself or her past? Perhaps he was imagining her to be a drug smuggler, a striptease artist, a mud wrestler, a call girl. Thinking that, her lips curved upward in a slight smile.

"There's no use testing me," he declared. "I won't ask you why you're smiling so mysteriously.''

"That's fine, because I have no intention of asking you how you knew I was smiling. It's blacker than pitch out here.''

"There you go again. I refuse to ask what pitch is.''

"Don't fret. I'll tell you anyway. It's tar. At least, I think it is.''

They were at her small cabin much too soon. "I'd ask you in," she said softly, "but I do need to call it a night.''

"That's okay. Perhaps another time before I leave. Thanks for helping with the fish. They were delicious even if they were ill-gotten gain.''

He walked her to the cabin door and was suddenly much too close for comfort. She was aware of his overwhelming masculinity, of his self-assured attractiveness, of everything about him. He bent his face toward hers, and she knew he meant to kiss her. She did not try to stop the action. This evening was pretend and fantasy anyway. One good-night kiss could do no harm, could only enhance the fantasy. His lips were firm but gentle. They demanded nothing she couldn't give. Even though his touch was light, she trembled slightly. Feeling the tremble, he murmured her name and pulled her into his arms, holding her against him, swaying with a slight motion such as one would use in comforting a small child. Reaching up, cupping his face with her hands, she felt its firm contours and wished she could see him. Moonless nights weren't to her liking. He kissed her again, less gently, and she swayed against him, lips parting beneath the pressure of his.

A natural sensuality, dormant and suppressed for so very long, began to bud, spreading a delicious, disturbing warmth over her entire being. It was only a good-night kiss, only a natural ending to an evening two people had shared amiably, yet it was a rarity to Lynn, something she hadn't let happen often. She let her arms steal around his neck, let her fingers know the feel of the warm flesh at the back of his neck and of the thick, healthy hair. Perhaps it was more her fault than his that the kiss flowed from the realm of the near-innocent into the very center of the storm. Without a will of her own, she felt her body melt and press against his.

When she felt Dan's hands travel to her hips and heard his breath coming in heavy rasps, a sense of panic replaced passion and enabled her to pull back from him.

"That's a very dangerous way to say good night," he whispered huskily.

"I know," she replied, unable to look at him directly, knowing her wildfire response had been more like an invitation than a parting. "I'm sorry. I really don't know what possessed me."

"Oh, don't be sorry," he said, touching a fingertip lightly against her smooth cheek. "I enjoyed every moment. Will you let me take you out somewhere tomorrow night? A real date—one where you won't have to work."

Inexplicable tears filled Lynn's eyes, flooding her with a mixture of indignation and self-disgust. "No, Dan," she replied quickly. "I don't think we can sustain tonight's experience through another evening."

"Seems to me we've found a satisfactory replacement," he murmured, bending to let his lips nuzzle against her throat.

She pulled back too abruptly for politeness. "I think this is a game more dangerous than the one of questions and answers would be. Good night."

Instead of pursuing the subject, as she had half expected him to do, Dan stepped away and said, "Good night then, Lynn. Sleep well."

Although his tone sounded perfectly natural, Lynn suspected irony behind the words. She was destined not to sleep well and he was probably quite aware of that.

Too long alone.

She stood on the wooden porch outside her door and watched until the beam from Dan's flashlight disappeared and he became one with the night. All the forest sounds seemed to close in around her: each bird's call, each branch bending in the breeze seemed to repeat that plaintive refrain, reverberating against her consciousness.

Too long alone.

Chapter Three

THE NEXT DAY passed, as did the one after that. Lynn wasn't sure enough of her own emotions to know if her feeling was closer to disappointment or relief at not hearing from Daniel Ross. She would be very relieved when he left the St. Clair area, for the ambivalence that had warred within her since their first meeting was getting to be unbearable.

How keenly she remembered that smug feeling of peace and contentment she had had while walking in the woods with Paddy. From the moment she had heard the first discordantly sung bars of "Shenandoah," she hadn't been quite the same. Ever since then Lynn had been wondering if she hadn't merely been living like a small animal burrowed into its hole beneath a rock. Safe from life, from love, from pain. So safe that some might argue that what she was doing wasn't living but existing.

She was not in love with Dan Ross, of course. She had barely met the man and knew nothing about him—and that was exactly what he knew about her. Yet he had managed to stir within her a feeling of discontent, a desire to have the unattainable. If she hadn't been a reasonable person, she would have resented him for these feelings. Being a reasonable person, she realized he had nothing to do with her disturbed psyche.

It was three evenings from the one she had spent with Dan. They were well counted in her mind, as unmistakable as if she had notched them there as the Indians notched trees to mark time. Soon he would be gone. She was glad for that. As long as he resided at the Wicklein place, she knew all either of them had to do was step across the posted boundaries to be face to face. When he was back in some unknown town or city in Illinois, then she could breathe more easily. Perhaps it would even be possible to settle down in her rut once more with some degree of recaptured peace.

The air was hot and oppressive, so after work she changed into old shorts and a loose cotton shirt, remaining barefoot. It was much too warm even to consider heating the cabin any more by cooking. Lynn rummaged through the refrigerator and withdrew a head of lettuce and other garden vegetables to chop up for a salad.

When she heard a knock on the front door, her heart made a curiously joyful jump, yet her mind was more reluctant to acknowledge such joy. She had no doubt who knocked. It wouldn't be Kim or Julie or anyone else from St. Clair standing there when she opened the door. She knew this more from intuition than intellect.

"Hi, pretty lady," Dan said brightly, smiling that smile she was beginning to know all too well. Yet he didn't seem supremely confident. There was an air of hesitation about him that seemed to plead with her not to dismiss him from her premises. "I've crossed your property line again without permission," he added.

"Some people never learn," she said, standing aside to let him enter her cabin. With a sweeping gaze, his keen gray eyes perceived her habitat. The little cabin was crude in many ways, but it was distinctly a woman's cabin. It was crowded, perhaps overly so, with all sorts of items she had liked too much to offer for sale in The Calico Cat.

The parquet floor was liberally sprinkled with rag and latch-hooked rugs, and the papered walls were almost completely covered with pictures and hangings.

"Is there a place to put this?" he asked, holding out an oval-shaped wicker basket filled to the brim with exotically colored wild flowers.

Bewildered more by Dan's presence than anything else, Lynn

looked about helplessly. Reaching out, she took the basket from his hands and tenderly touched the golden petals of the black-eyed susans. "Thank you so much, Dan. They're lovely."

"Oh, I don't really deserve thanks. Technically, they're Jess's flowers, were growing in his garden. But I decided they'd probably be dead by the time he gets back down here, so you might as well have them."

Lynn hid her smile by burying her face in the bouquet as if to take in its aroma, then moved some objects about on a table to make room for the basket. By his manner, she could tell Dan did believe these were flowers planted in a garden instead of wild flowers—wild flowers that many people considered weeds. Personally, she loved them all: the Queen Anne's lace and all the little yellow and purple blossoms that huddled close against the earth's bosom.

"Is the basket Jess's, too?" she asked, feigning innocence.

"Of course not," he replied indignantly. "Most people think I have an honest face, and you're practically accusing me of thievery. I bought that basket in town from some crowded, overpriced little shop. I asked to speak to the owner or manager to complain about the prices, but the clerk told me she'd gone to the bank on business. So I thought what the heck, and bought the thing anyway. Who knows, perhaps it's a special sort of basket such as those sold at the Smithsonian. And you're a special sort of person."

"I'm sorry I missed you when you were in," she said with a small smile. "No one mentioned it."

"Are you going to ask me to sit down, or do I have to keep standing here and looking awkward?"

"Actually, I had thought we had the understanding we weren't to do this again. But since you're here, you might as well stay for supper. If you can survive on a salad, that is. I don't have air conditioning in here and it's much too hot to cook."

"A salad's fine. I'd eat a combination of arsenic and ground glass as long as you'll let me stay."

While Lynn prepared the salad ingredients and tossed them

together, they made light conversation. Finally, she met his gaze directly and said, "I guess I seem awfully odd to you."

"Odd? No, not really. I must admit you arouse my curiosity, but I'm sure you have a good reason for your secrecy. And I'm not asking you to divulge any information, but there is something I want to tell you about myself. We don't know each other well, but I enjoy your company immensely, and I'd like to keep in touch with you. In order to do this, I need to tell you . . ."

With a wary shake of her head, Lynn managed to prevent him from saying more. "You're leaving soon, Dan. I've enjoyed being with you, too, but it can't go beyond that and I can't explain. If you start telling me your secrets, then I'll feel lousy because I won't tell mine. So let's leave it as it is. Though I'm not sure how we'll make it through the rest of the evening. I suppose we can still discuss religion and politics. That's about all we didn't cover the other night."

He smiled slightly. "I think we'll find our own forms of diversion."

When she shot him a skeptical, warning look, he laughed heartily. "I left the diversion out on the porch. After we eat, I'll bring it in."

"Now you have me curious," she admitted, picking at the salad without much appetite.

After they had eaten and done the dishes, he made a great production of withdrawing to her porch to bring in his surprise. Lynn laughed out loud when he came back in bearing an old Scrabble game which he had probably unearthed from Jess Wicklein's closet. They acted as carefree and giddy as a pair of kids while they played the game with a great spirit of competitiveness. When they were each down to the last few tiles and the score was very close, Lynn looked around the room while she was waiting for Dan to see if he could play or if he had to pass. How strange, she thought. It was quite dark in the cabin and, with daylight saving's time, dark didn't come until a bit after nine o'clock and she knew it couldn't be that late.

"Ah hah," Dan exclaimed triumphantly, slipping a combination of unlikely consonants into place on the board.

Just when Lynn was ready to challenge his word, knowing he was ready for the challenge, because BYZQ was all too obviously a playful fabrication, the thunder began to roll.

"Oh, boy," she said, "so that's where all this heat and humidity's been leading. I think we're in for a thunderstorm. You better head for home or you may be stuck for a while."

"No way. Not when I was on the verge of winning. Besides, isn't there some advantage to being together in a thunderstorm? I'd rather be frightened here with you than scared stiff all alone at the other place. You have to remember that I'm a city slicker and not accustomed to all these raw elements."

Lynn didn't attempt to argue the point. She merely turned on the lights, challenged BYZQ, made him back down, and went on to win the game by only three points.

"Now I wish I'd gone home," he remarked, sticking out his lower lip in a pretend pout.

"You had your chance. Let's go out and see what the sky looks like."

"Can you tell things by looking at the sky, pretty lady?"

"A few things. Not a lot. But it never hurts to look."

Outside the atmosphere was definitely stormy. From a distance away, the lightning zigzagged across the sky.

"Tornado conditions," she said.

"Really? How can you tell?"

She shrugged. "It's just a feeling. Or maybe it's a memory from having seen it like this before. The look of the sky. The sound of the thunder. And feel the coolness in the air. When you came, it was blazing hot, and now I'm shivering. Watch the trees, Dan, when the lightning flashes again. You'll see that the leaves are blown in a funny way, so that the lighter undersides of them are showing."

"You trying to put a city feller on? Scare me for the fun of it?"

Lynn shook her head and laughed. "Chances are there will be

some rain mixed with a good deal of sound and fury. Maybe enough wind to break off a few tree limbs. I don't think there's ever been a really bad twister here.''

"You have a basement?''

Glancing at his strong, handsome profile as he studied the sky, Lynn smiled to herself. "Not really a basement. Kind of a root cellar or wine cellar sort of thing. But we would be safer there than out here or in the cabin itself if anything does develop.''

They watched the sky together until the rain began to fall in torrents blown by the wind. Slightly dampened, they ran back into the cabin. Just when they were discussing if they should start another Scrabble game or not, a crack of thunder seemed to rip the sky apart, then the cabin went dark.

"How about that,'' Lynn said lightly. "I do believe the electrical lines were just knocked out.''

"Don't you think maybe we should go to your cellar?'' Dan asked nervously.

Lynn found his anxiety somehow touching. Most men would have put up some kind of front to preserve a macho image. Not Dan Ross. Honest and straightforward, he admitted being slightly afraid of a possible tornado.

"It probably won't be any worse,'' she told him gently, "than any summer storm in Illinois.''

"I know,'' he said with a sigh, "but out here, you seem so much closer to it.''

"Anyway, I'd better hunt out the candles and matches so that we can see what we're doing.''

After she had supplied Dan with candles of various shapes and sizes, Lynn slipped back out to the porch for a look. The sky was definitely dark and ominous. There was a strange quietness in the air. She lived so far out that she knew she wouldn't be able to hear the civil defense siren if it blew, and she didn't own a transistor radio. The wind blew harder, making an eerie sound, and she shivered with a feeling that went deeper than the touch of chilled air on her skin.

"Bring the candles, Daniel. We're going to the cellar," she announced as lightly as possible, scooping Paddy into her arms. For once the little dog behaved impeccably.

Dan followed her down the dark, narrow steps into the small room, which the three of them seemed to fill completely. Somehow, as they burrowed there, they seemed far away from everything and everyone. Above them and around them the storm continued to rage. They could hear the water pelting against the sides of the cabin. With the solemnity of very small children, Dan and Lynn arranged four of the candles to light their cobweb-laden haven as well as possible. There were no seats, so they sat side by side on the bottom step while Paddy stretched out quietly at their feet. When their knees touched, Lynn didn't mind. There were times when the nearness of another human being was extremely nice. This was one of those times.

"Something about this reminds me of being a kid," Dan said. "This was the sort of atmosphere we set up to tell ghost stories."

One thing led to another and they started telling each other ghost stories remembered from many years before. Instead of growing scared, however, they grew giggly. By the time Dan completed his last tale, Lynn was laughing so hard her sides were aching. Apparently he was so intent on entertaining her that he forgot all about his nervousness at the storm.

"Listen," she said when she was finally able to quit laughing, "I think it must be over. The worst of it anyway."

"You think it's safe to go up and see if you still have a house up there?"

"I think it's safe. I also think we can assume I have a house up there. Surely we would have heard if all the logs and glass had come crashing down."

"Not necessarily. I had you mesmerized with terror at my stories of bloody fingers."

Once outside, they watched the sky again, with Paddy seeming to look upward with dark, questioning eyes.

"It's over and done, Paddy boy," Lynn said reassuringly. "A little more wind, a little more rain, but the fury of the storm is spent. Now we can rest."

"I suppose I should go home and see to things there," Dan said reluctantly, "but I hate to leave you with no lights or anything."

"That doesn't matter," she replied. "It isn't likely to be fixed till morning. I'll be okay. But you're welcome to stay for a while if you like. It isn't late. How about some cake and milk? Now that the air has cooled, I find that the salad didn't fill me up."

"Sounds great."

They ate and drank by the light of the flickering, mismatched candles that were gradually melting down into nothingness, molten droplets forming on the surfaces beneath them.

Lynn watched Dan's face, its strong lines softened by the changing flickers of light. He looked so very familiar. She had been with him only a few times, yet it was as if she had known him forever. Perhaps she was overripe for friendship, for love, for a close human encounter of any sort. Yet she could not quite believe all of her feeling was due to whim, because the rapport they had found seemed so special. She knew nothing of him and he knew nothing of her, yet she had the peculiar feeling that they knew each other better in some ways than most people ever knew each other.

"Two dollars for your thoughts," Dan said softly.

"I like a man who keeps up with the times, who is well-aware that a penny would never part me from my thoughts."

"But the two dollars would?"

Smiling wistfully, she replied, "I suppose I was just thinking about us. About this entire, insane relationship of ours. I met you, yelled at you, told you I wanted nothing to do with you. And I end up frying the fish you caught in my river, hiding you in my cellar during a near tornado, and feeding you chocolate cake by candlelight."

"And you won't even let me tell you who—"

40

"Shhh," she whispered, touching a finger lightly against his lips. "Don't bring it up again. Let's keep it the way it is. We've already agreed there is no future for us, so let's retain the element of mystery. We can keep the memory of the time we've had together. Take it out on lonely, cloudy days and maybe smile a bit. I don't want it spoiled by—"

"By the truth? Can the truth really be that harmful? If we discuss the obstacles, maybe we could overcome them."

"No, Dan. Believe me. Mine can't be overcome." She pushed back her chair and got up, moving briskly about the small kitchen. "Would you like another piece of cake?"

"No, thank you. The problem I have at the moment isn't one that can be overcome by cake, avoidance, jokes, or another game of Scrabble."

Noting his heavy, sober tone, Lynn walked toward the living room. She wanted him to go away right now. She wanted that very badly. They had had a few moments of fun and pleasure. If he wanted more, that was too bad. After all, he had been forewarned that nothing else was possible.

"Want Paddy to go home with you for protection from the dark and stormy night?" she asked lightly, hoping to avert him from any serious conversation.

"Won't you just sit and talk with me awhile, Lynn, before I go? As you said, it really isn't late. And you can't read or watch TV."

Lynn let her body sink slowly onto the sofa. She moved slowly. To an onlooker, she might have appeared quite casual, but every muscle was pulled taut. The candles had been left in the kitchen, and their glow wasn't bright enough to touch the living room with much light.

Dan sat at the other end of the sofa, circumspectly away from her. When he spoke, he didn't look at her but at the dark window from which nothing could be seen. "I've never been a romantic, Lynn. I've always been much too practical to believe in love at first sight and all that sort of thing. In fact, I often think I'm too practical to believe in love."

41

"Dan, please don't . . ."

"Just let me finish this much, my dear. I was married once. We were very young. Too young, really. I don't suppose either of us knew what marriage involved. Maybe it would have lasted, maybe not. I like to think it would have, but Cara was killed in an auto accident a few weeks before our first anniversary."

"I'm so sorry." The words seemed inadequate, yet there were not really any words that suited such an occasion.

"What Cara and I had was special, even if we weren't much more than kids. After the bitterness and pain had worn off, I guess I more or less expected to fall in love again someday. Well, it never happened. After a while I didn't expect it. I decided love was for the very young, the very idealistic. I hadn't completely ruled out the idea of remarrying at some point, because I'd like to have a home and children, yet no woman ever seemed to evoke any sort of special feeling in me. Not until now."

Deliberately making her voice hard, Lynn replied, "Then don't start being a romantic now, Dan. Not with me. And I'd advise you to ward off such feelings on short acquaintance with any woman. It takes time for real emotion to grow, to see if it will last."

"Do you deny a special sort of feeling when we're together?"

By the light of the dimly burning candles, Lynn viewed his strongly chiseled profile. Special? Sure, he was special. He had the looks, humor, and charisma to be any woman's fantasy. And she was a lonely woman who had lots of fantasies and little in the way of reality. Just to be with him was to be somehow perched on the brink of danger. A step backward and she'd be safe, a step forward and she would plunge into the unknown.

"I don't deny that. But, be honest, we set out to make it that way. This was a vacation for us both, a bit of playacting, a bit of fantasy. And think about it for a moment, how it all came about. If, when we had first met, I'd acted all chatty and cozy and filled you in on my boring past and let you know how attractive and witty I think you are and how my goal was to marry and have three children and a house in the suburbs, you would have gone running back to Illinois without giving me a second thought."

He laughed huskily and finally turned to look at her. It was better when he hadn't, she thought. Those eyes had a mystical power over her.

"Are you trying to tell me, kid, that I've fallen victim to the playing-hard-to-get game?"

"Not exactly. Because it isn't a game. But it *is* human nature to want what we can't have, to desire the unattainable. All I'm saying is that this element of mystery, this cloak-and-dagger routine, has lent a special flavor to our relationship. So I wouldn't go making proclamations of love, Dan. This feeling we have probably wouldn't stand the test of time."

"Probably, you say. Yet you're not about to give us a chance to find out. Can't you trust me enough to tell me your terrible secret? I know, I know. I've promised not to ask. But I do so much want to see you again, want to know you better, want to see if we can endure this test of time you mention."

To her dismay, tears filled her eyes, trembled on her long lashes, and overflowed onto her cheeks. It had been a mistake to accept his first invitation and an even bigger one to invite him in tonight. Fantasies are nice while they last, but if they're too nice, then pain sets in when the fantasy ends.

"Hey," he said softly, spotting the tears and moving over beside her, "I'm so sorry, Lynn. You tried to be honest with me and I went and broke my promise." He touched her cheek softly, a fingertip grazing lightly over the slight moisture there. A strange sound escaped her throat, a sob that was trying not to form. Dan pulled her into his arms, pressing her head against his chest, letting his hands move about in her long, thick hair, fingers tangling in the dark tendrils.

This time she knew what to expect when she lifted her face and looked into his eyes. He kissed her slowly, tenderly, until the blood turned to molten lava in her veins. She had waited so long to know the feel of such a kiss, had lain awake so many

43

nights wondering what it would be like. And now Dan was here with her, holding her in a way that made her want to cry out for more.

"Oh Lord, Lynn, I love the feel of you. So soft, so sweet, so good within my arms. Love me, sweetheart, love me."

Not really having any choice, Lynn moved to hold him more tightly in her arms. Knowing she should pull back, she did not, she could not. His power over her was too great for that.

Just when his hands moved reverently to touch the smooth skin beneath her shirt, the lights all came on with a blinding effect. Shocked back into sensibility, Lynn felt her cheeks burn hotly with shame.

Cursing softly beneath his breath, Dan let her move away from him. With a rueful look, he said, "I don't suppose it would do any good for me to suggest we turn off the lights and take up where we left off when so rudely interrupted."

Lynn looked at him, cheeks still high with color. "You must really think a lot of me now. I tell you there can be no future for us, then nearly take you for a tumble on the couch."

Daring to reach out and touch the spot of red on her left cheek, Dan smiled a slow, sweet smile. "I think as much of you as I ever did. And maybe even more. If we get carried away when we embrace, Lynn, it's because our feeling is special. No matter how hard you try to deny that. I freely admit it's special for me. I've never let myself lose control like that, yet I would have taken you if it hadn't been for those blasted lights. Why does the electric company have to be so efficient?"

She couldn't help laughing softly at his obvious frustration. "You're asking me to believe you didn't make love to other women?"

"I've had sex with other women," he said bluntly. "After being sure we're free from the dangers of pregnancy, disease, and emotional commitments."

"Sounds rather cold and clinical."

"But safe. And satisfactory. Up until now, that is. Lynn, I—"

"Please, no more. I can't take it. Tonight, a few minutes ago, I wouldn't have stopped you. I would have been yours in any way you wanted me. I'm not particularly proud of that. I have, by necessity, led a lonely life, and you're a very special man, Daniel Ross. I could easily love you. Probably, in some peculiar, incomprehensibly impossible way, I do love you. And if we had become one, made love, then I suppose I would have loved you all the more. But soon you would still have to leave, and I couldn't go with you and I can't let you come back. If we become any more at all to each other, then I'll have to tell you . . . well, what I haven't told you. And then it would end anyway. So let it be now. Just let it be."

Embarassment and shame were replaced by simple grief, and Lynn didn't even try to hide the silent tears that rolled down her face. Never had she felt so vulnerable.

He gave a deep sigh that was almost like a shudder, the force of it shaking his broad chest and shoulders. "Oh, Lynn, don't be ashamed because our feelings got out of control. You're a woman with natural needs and inclinations, and we've shared some rare moments together. I could never see you as cheap or easy. Goodness shines from your eyes as brightly as the sun. But I don't want to say good-bye to you. And by that I don't mean I'm asking to spend the night. Just let me keep in touch. Please."

The pleading in his voice was almost more than her heart could bear. Within her there was a tiny hope that maybe her past would not matter to this man. Maybe it would be safe to tell him she was Linda Marshall, daughter of Davy Marshall, and that the FBI and various gangsters still wanted to ask her a lot of questions. Surely somewhere on earth there had to be *someone* to whom it made no difference. Why couldn't that someone be Dan Ross? It was worth a chance, wasn't it? Sure, she'd feel pain if he backed off from her for that reason, but she was feeling pain anyway at the idea of never seeing him again.

Before she had a chance to respond, he spoke again. "Lynn, I have to tell you this. I'll feel terrible if I leave here without it, and I won't let you stop me this time. My name isn't Ross, it's Resnick. I was just telling everyone Ross to avoid publicity while I was here for rest. Most of the time I'm mobbed with people, and I badly needed this time to be alone and be just-plain-Joe."

For a few moments, his words didn't register. When they did, the impact was terrific.

"Daniel Resnick," she said slowly. "Senator Daniel Resnick."

"Yeah," he said, hanging his head sheepisly, "that's me."

She threw back her head, feeling that she should laugh or cry, but her eyes and throat both felt very dry. "I feel foolish at not having recognized you. Senator from my neighboring state, a face often seen on television and in the papers, and I don't even recognize you. Well, congratulations, Senator Resnick. You're one of the few people who looks even better in person than in your publicity photos."

Apparently hearing the bitter edge to her words, Dan said quickly, "I tried to tell you, Lynn. I tried a long time ago. As soon as I saw how special you were, how much I wanted to be with you, I wanted it all out in the open."

All out in the open, she thought bitterly. Just when she had been spinning a pretty daydream, he put the kiss of death on any hope of a future for them. Even if he nobly exclaimed her past made no difference to him, she knew it would. This man was strongly mentioned as a possible presidential candidate—if not for this next election, then most certainly for the one after that. He was popular, fair, honest. No hint of scandal or corruption had ever touched him. Senator Daniel Resnick was the kind of leader the country needed, and becoming involved with the daughter of a gang leader was not exactly what would do him the most good. She didn't try to kid herself that she could be seen in public with him and still be known as Lynn Marsh. Any woman seen with him would attract attention, and it wouldn't take someone in the news media long to ferret out the truth.

"I'm not angry, Dan," she said gently. "I know I wouldn't let you speak when you wanted to. But please go now. And don't ever come back. If you have any feelings for me at all, then just do that."

"I wish I could understand." He held his hands out, palms upward in a gesture of helplessness. His face was filled with despair, and she wanted nothing more than to take him in her arms to ease the confusion and pain.

"You can't. You just have to trust my judgment. What you've told me has convinced me even more that there can be no future for us. We've had this bit of time together. Let's remember it always as a good time. Please, Dan, please. Just leave. And don't look back."

"That's what you want?"

"That's what I want," she repeated after him, knowing it wasn't *want*. It was necessity.

"Good-bye, my love. If you ever change your mind, I suppose you can find me. Most people seem to be able to."

She nodded, unable to speak. Dan turned and walked away. As she had asked, he did not look back. She watched until he was out of sight, but that didn't take long because it was dark outside and his legs moved in long, easy strides across the wooded area.

"Oh, Paddy, Paddy, why did this have to happen?" she asked, hugging the little beagle to her. Seeming to understand, he did not resist her affection but snuggled against her, letting her wet his sleek hair with tears that came as forcefully as the storm that had so recently passed their way.

Once, just a few days ago, she had told herself that a little bit of time in his company could do no harm, just create a pleasant diversion from the rut into which she had fallen. And now? Now that rut seemed such a wonderful place, and she longed to be happily within its confines once more. Daniel Resnick had given her a taste of what love, life, and happiness could be, and then she had had to send him away—for his sake and for her own.

Why, oh, why? It would have been so much simpler if he had been a butcher, a baker, a candlestickmaker. Any of those just might have been able to handle Linda Marshall. But not a senator with aspirations for the presidency.

No way.

It really didn't seem fair that fate had played this trick on her. But she had learned a long time ago that life isn't fair.

Lynn tidied the house and went to bed. Before she drifted off to sleep, she thought of Dan. Asleep, she dreamed of him. When she awoke, he was the first thing on her mind, so real she could almost feel the pressure of his lips on hers, hear the hearty sound of his laughter touching against her ears. She had a feeling that it was going to be a very long time before she didn't think of him. Maybe forever.

Chapter Four

DURING THE NEXT few weeks, Senator Daniel Resnick of Illinois probably wasn't in the news any more often than he ever had been. It was simply that Lynn now noticed the news items, where she had dismissed them with a casual reading before she had met Dan. Her inner excitement was something over which she had no control. When she picked up a St. Louis or Springfield newspaper, she couldn't relax and read the news and features until she had rapidly turned the pages in search of any mention of him.

Occasionally his picture was in the paper, and looking at him, even in black and white press photos that weren't terribly good, caused a quickening of her heart. A time or two she had even seen him on the television news. Because of that, the news shows suddenly became her favorite programs, and she sat glued in front of the television screen every evening at six o'clock and again at ten o'clock with the avid attention of a soap opera fan.

It was silly. In fact, it was an adolescent mode of behavior. With her intellect, Lynn realized that. With another part of her that had nothing to do with rationality, she didn't care. Even when she had been in her early teens, she hadn't been prone to yearning over screen idols, getting crushes on teachers, or pasting mementoes in scrapbooks. So why now? There was only one possible answer to that question: Dan was special.

"You're awfully quiet these days," Julie observed one day during a slow time in the shop.

Lynn paused in her dusting and rearranging of shelves and

merchandise. "Am I? I guess we've been so busy lately that I've forgotten what it's like to have slow days when we can chat."

"Boy, it *has* been busy," the young girl exclaimed, pushing back her thatch of fair hair. "Kim and I'll be back in school before long. How on earth are you going to manage then? I mean, I can still come after school and on Saturdays some if you want, but I don't see how you can handle it by yourself all day long."

With a smile, Lynn said, "You forget that the business of The Calico Cat is mostly seasonal, Julie. There will only be a few days in between the time school starts and the Labor Day weekend. After that, it really slacks off in here."

"Yeah, I guess I forgot about that since I didn't work here last summer. You ever get bored in here in the winter?"

"Sure. But not very often. Things pick up a bit around Christmastime, and after that I do a lot of my repairs, remodeling, ordering, and bookkeeping. Those things are important, and there simply isn't time during the tourist season to do anything except what's totally necessary. But sometimes on cold, snowy days, I stay home. There are a few advantages to a seasonal business—and to being my own boss."

"That would be neat," Julie agreed, "to look out the window some awful, gray day and just say 'Heck, I'm not going to work today.' "

"It's also a practical decision at times. Of course, I can't do it often if I hope to stay in business and have a reputation of being reliable, but there are times when it doesn't make sense to risk life and limb to get here through the snow drifts and burn precious fuel to heat the shop. Not *that* many people will get out in a blizzard to buy a shell ashtray or a macrame hanging basket."

"Or a decorated milk can," the blonde teenager giggled. "Remember that fat lady who was in here earlier this summer who wasn't going to buy it until that man acted like he was dying to get his hands on it? Gosh, he was cute. Did you know him, Lynn?"

Being careful to keep her face averted so her assistant couldn't read it easily, Lynn replied, "I had met him. He was down here vacationing, was borrowing or renting the Wicklein place."

"He didn't really want that milk can, did he?"

"No, of course not. He was just one of those people who's completely uninhibited and has a wild sense of humor."

"Gosh, of all the rotten luck. On vacation, huh? No wonder I haven't seen him since."

"Have you been looking?" Lynn asked with a laugh.

The girl shrugged her shoulders. "Oh, not actively. But you don't forget a hunk like that easily. You might know someone who looks that good doesn't hang around St. Clair on a permanent basis."

Still not glancing directly at Julie, Lynn continued the conversation as casually as possible. "He was much too old for you anyway, Julie."

"But a girl can dream," she said with a sigh. "Can't you just imagine having a guy that good-looking knock at your door to pick you up for a date?"

Lynn smiled down at the collection of porcelain ornaments she was dusting. He *had* knocked at her door. He had held her, kissed her, and nearly overwhelmed her. But she didn't voice any of that to Julie. Instead, she said, "Can't you just imagine your father's reaction if a guy that age came to pick you up? I doubt that he would be impressed by how cute he was."

Julie giggled again, evidently picturing her overprotective father confronting a boyfriend of hers who was nearly as old as he was. "Oh, well. A girl can dream. If you're going to fantasize, you might as well fantasize big. That's what I always say."

"You always say that, do you?"

"Well, honestly, Lynn, now admit it: did *you* think he was good-looking?"

She was saved from answering the question by the tinkling of the bell over the door which signaled the entry of a customer. It wasn't that Lynn minded chatting with Julie or even that she minded admitting Dan was handsome. Any fool could see that. However, Lynn knew that Julie, despite her youth and giddiness, was a perceptive girl and might easily guess from Lynn's

51

manner that Dan was more to her than a mysterious stranger who had sauntered into The Calico Cat one day, then disappeared forever.

His abrupt appearance in her life had had an unsettling effect. Try as she would, she hadn't been able yet to recapture the comfortable feeling of early summer. The old saying that it was better to have loved and lost than never to have loved at all came to mind. She wasn't certain she agreed with that. Maybe it was true in the case of a couple who had years together and many memories to share. But what had she and Dan had? A few meetings, a few conversations, a few caresses. It was only enough to let her know she was kidding herself about not needing a family, a close friend, a love. She had been on the earth a quarter of a century and the only living thing she had that she felt free to hug and love was fat funny little Paddy.

One day flowed into another with a sameness Lynn found both irritating and depressing. When compared to the haunted and harassed life Linda Marshall had lived a few years ago, the peace of a solitary existence running a small business in a small town had seemed marvelous. And, of course, she wouldn't go back to that terrible time. All the same, she admitted to herself that her complacence would probably never fully return.

Nothing had changed, really. The shop had busy days and slow days. Some customers were crabby and others were totally wonderful. In the distant sort of way that was necessary for her, she had many friends among the townspeople and regular visitors to the St. Clair area. In her free time, she still strolled through the woods and sat at the edge of the river, sometimes taking a swim while Paddy yapped at her from the bank. She still sat at the old, scarred desk in the little office at the back of the store and made out orders and paid bills. Once, on a hot, lazy Sunday, she even went canoeing with Julie, Kim, and a few of their friends. The summer was nearly identical to the past few summers she had spent in the green hills and valleys of the Ozarks.

If nothing had changed, why was everything so very different? Lynn wasn't actually grieving. She didn't have a deep, hopeless feeling. She often laughed and chatted with people and enjoyed the small happenings of life, but it somehow seemed as if she were going through motions that had no real meaning or purpose. Something was missing. She had youth, health, independence, serenity. While Lynn knew she was lucky in many ways, she couldn't help but regret the string of too many lonely hours.

Everyone she met seemed to have *someone*, even if that someone was very far away. It was a curious feeling to be filling out a card or form and to look at the line that said IN CASE OF EMERGENCY, PLEASE NOTIFY: and not know what to put in the blank that followed. Usually she ended up listing the name and number of whatever girl happened to be working in The Calico Cat at that particular time. Who would sit beside the bed if she were injured or had a heart attack? Who would arrange the funeral if she died?

This is ridiculous, she thought. It didn't matter. Until lately, she had scarcely ever considered such things. With the world as big as it was, there must certainly be lots of people with no relatives and few close friends. It hadn't been a problem before, and it didn't need to be one now.

The Saturday evening before Labor Day Lynn locked the door behind the last customer and drew a deep sigh of relief.

"Terrific day, huh, Lynn?" observed Kim.

'Was it ever,'' she agreed, kicking off her shoes while she cleared out the cash register. "Today was so busy *and* profitable that it makes me wonder if I should keep the place open on Monday. I could make a killing with it being the last major holiday of the season.''

The teenagers exchanged anxious glances and Lynn laughed. "Go on home, both of you. I was only kidding. None of the other shops or offices in St. Clair will be open. And I wouldn't ask you to work anyway. You gave up your Saturday to help me out, now run and enjoy the next two days.''

Kim and Julie headed toward the door with hastily mumbled words of parting. Kim went on out and Julie, the more thoughtful of the two girls, looked back at Lynn. "Would you want to come to my house tomorrow evening? It's just a family barbecue. No big deal, but I'm sure my folks would love to have you and . . ."

"Thanks, Julie," Lynn said softly. "That's very nice of you, but I have other plans, and I wouldn't inflict myself on your family on such short notice. Have a good time, though."

Julie nodded and went on out of the shop with a reluctance that let Lynn know Julie realized she did not really have other plans. The girls must know, even if they didn't ask, that she lived all by herself and was never seen running around town with anyone at all.

Shaking her head to rid it of incipient melancholia, she firmly turned her attention back to tallying the day's receipts and making up the bank deposit. When that was done, she slipped her shoes back on and stood up. After turning out most of the lights, she picked up the blue vinyl pouch and went outside into the sweltering heat. She locked the door from the outside and shook it to make sure it was secure. She walked down the sidewalk to the bank, which was only a block and a half from her store, and placed the vinyl pouch in the night depository. Then she returned to The Calico Cat, for her little Triumph Spitfire was parked near the rear entrance.

The wariness she had learned living in St. Louis and in Paris had gradually worn off. She had felt no fear when walking down the street holding an unconcealed bank pouch. Darkness was approaching, and she wasn't worried at all as she headed toward the back of the store to get into her car alone. In all the time that she had lived in St. Clair, she could not recall a single murder, rape, or robbery. Nearly all the violence that occurred in the area turned out to be domestic in origin, and that was one worry Lynn didn't have: no jealous boyfriend, no ill-tempered husband who drank too much on a Saturday night.

Without really thinking, she reached down with her key and unlocked the door.

The deep, male laughter floated up out of nowhere. She would have known that laughter anywhere, any time. Her pulse was pounding wildly and she was rendered speechless. Turning helplessly, she found herself face to face with Dan Resnick.

"Don't tell me, Lynn Marsh, that you actually locked your car."

"I . . . I guess it's just a habit. I didn't stop to think."

"And not only did you lock it, you used the key to unlock it. I can't believe that."

Feeling foolish and flustered, Lynn looked down at the British green car with the black and white houndstooth check upholstery. "The top is down, isn't it?"

"Very much so," he said with a grin. "Anyone could reach right in and push the door lock. Or they wouldn't have to bother. They could just do this."

With a sudden move, he had leaped neatly into the small car to sit in the passenger's seat. Lynn stood there on the other side of the car staring down at him, still not sure he was really there and still not knowing what to say.

"Where did you come from, Dan?" she asked, the question making her feel more foolish than ever. Glancing about, she explained, "I mean, I don't see a car or a suitcase or anything."

"Will you get in?" he requested softly.

Nodding, she sat down behind the steering wheel and looked at him, her hands folded in her lap like an obedient little girl's.

"Really, aren't you going to explain?"

He smiled. She had thought she remembered that smile, but she hadn't. Not really.

"Who needs a car or a suitcase? I came by magic carpet. This genie came to me and said, 'Hey, senator, what's the matter with you these days? You're as mopey and grumpy as an old man.' And I said, 'Genie, there's this brown-eyed girl down in Missouri who lingers in my mind in an impossible sort of way. Even though I've only known her a little while and haven't seen her for ever so long, the thought of her won't go away.' "

"Dan," she warned.

He took one finger and placed it across her lips. "Rule one is that you never ever interrupt a senator when he's speaking. There's always a chance, if you listen for a century or two, that he might say something worth hearing. Now, to continue. This

55

genie told me that I had only one wish and that I'd better make it a good one. I told him that I wanted to wish to be with you, but if that came true, you'd probably throw me out. Or dump me into the river. Something drastic, anyway.

"Well, this genie was a helpful sort. Told me he had a degree in psychology. What he said was, 'Senator, you should know by now that women always want the opposite of what they say.' Now, don't get upset, Lynn. I *know* that's a chauvinistic statement, but this genie was an old-fashioned sort, being older than Father Time. I didn't want to upset him by pointing out that men are quite as likely as women to be illogical, because that could well have cost me my wish."

When he paused for breath, Lynn attempted to interrupt between gasps of laughter.

"Woman," he said sternly, "will you cease and desist and let me finish this tale? After all, the way I recall it, you *did* ask for an explanation. Anyway, I took a gamble that the genie was correct in this case—he seemed so terribly wise and kind—and so I said: 'I wish I was with Lynn.' Next thing I knew, I was being whisked up into the air on a magic carpet."

"Will you stop this nonsense and talk straight?" she said, but the sternness she intended to convey was lost because she was still shaking with giggles.

He looked directly at her, his face handsome and strong in the twilight, and seemed suddenly quite solemn. "Lynn, please, please tell me that genie was right. Tell me I'm crazy. Tell me we don't know each other at all. Tell me I'm not behaving like a grown man, let alone a fairly prominent politician. Tell me anything at all except that I was wrong."

She looked directly into his unwavering gray eyes and, in that moment, would have promised him the moon if it had been hers to give.

"You're making it so very hard for me," she said softly.

"Then you're going to throw me out?"

"Throwing you into the river sounds like a better idea."

"Getting wet must be your quaint idea of a greeting. It

seems to me that *you* ended up taking a dip the first time we met."

"You must be a glutton for punishment," she replied, giving a faint laugh at the memory of their first encounter, "to keep turning up when I've been so terribly rude and discouraging."

"That's me all right," Dan agreed cheerfully. "Somewhat of a masochist. Promise you won't tell my constituents?"

"I'm not going to tell anybody anything about you. Right now my only problem is what I'm going to tell *you*. Or do with you."

"We could go someplace more comfortable to talk," he suggested. "I don't have anything personal against this car, but it is a bit cramped and hot. And I could drink at least a gallon of anything cold without pausing for air."

"I can believe that. Anyone who can talk like you do must have an awfully good respiratory system."

"It's in the diaphragm, you know. Talking a lot is like singing, really. It takes training and practice. Think about it, Lynn. Who would vote for a man who is always gasping for air in the midst of important speeches?"

"You're impossible, Daniel Resnick."

"That's true. But I'm also lovable."

When she did not respond, he looked at her beseechingly. "Aren't I?"

Taking a deep breath, she said, "Yes. Yes, you are. Which makes it all the more difficult. Where did you have in mind that we should go to talk—this 'someplace more comfortable'?"

He stretched his long legs out in front of him as much as the Triumph would allow and answered, "Well, I can't exactly say 'your place or mine, baby' since I don't have a place. I turned my key to the Wicklein place back in to Jess and haven't seen him since."

"If you were smart, you would have had one made while you had it in your possession."

"But I'm much too honest for that. You know how politicians are, always taking oaths and whatnot."

"And breaking them and whatnot," she retorted wryly.

During the stream of chatter, Lynn was aware of a quaking sensation within her. She needed him. She needed him so very much. Did he have any idea what he was doing to her? Probably not. He might be confident enough to make an accurate guess at his physical effect on her but, without knowing her background, he couldn't know of the emotional upheaval, of the terrible inner battle she was fighting. *Keep it light. Keep it light.* That was what she kept telling herself, yet underneath the banter there was a current of feeling too strong and real to be denied.

"Are you one of those people who don't trust politicians?"

"I try to make my judgments of politicians on an individual basis, just as I do with everyone else," Lynn replied with mock solemnity.

"That could be a mistake. We're a tricky lot."

"You think I don't know that? I tell you to go away and not come back, and here you are in my car and I don't know what on earth I'm going to do with you. Really, Dan, how did you get here?"

"I hitched a ride with a friend who was coming this way for a vacation. Spur of the moment decision. I have a few days off. When I have to go back, I thought I might talk some pretty woman into giving me a ride to the airport in Springfield or St. Louis."

"No luggage?" she asked, not really believing this was happening.

"Only a little." He pointed over to the wall outside the back door of The Calico Cat where a dark leather suitcase stood all alone.

"I see."

"I'm not sure you do, Lynn." All the lightness was now gone from his voice. "I don't have any evil designs on your honor. I'll check into a motel."

"On Labor Day weekend in a tourist town without prior reservations? You've got to be kidding."

"I'll sleep in a pup tent outside. I'll sit up all night in the public park. Lynn, please, let's just talk. I'd like you to trust me enough to let me go to your place with you till we iron out a few wrinkles, but if you'd rather not, then anything else will do. If necessary, I'll do my talking across the table from you in a crowded restaurant.''

She placed her face in her upturned palms for a long moment, then glanced back at him and shook her head slowly. ''I don't think the wrinkles can be ironed out, Dan. They're permanent, and you're going to have to accept that. But, as for trusting you with my honor, that isn't a problem. I'm not afraid of you. Not at all. If anything, I'm afraid of myself.''

''If that's supposed to scare me off, forget it. Now, please, can we go talk?''

What was she supposed to do? Order him out of the Triumph and make him stand here on Second Street in St. Clair with his suitcase by his side? Against her better judgment, she placed the key in the ignition, pressed down the clutch, and turned the key. He retrieved his suitcase.

All the way across town, down the highway, and over the gravel road that led to her cabin, he kept up a stream of talk that was mostly nonsense. He said nothing serious, nothing weighty, nothing that had anything to do with futures or compromises or wild ideas of love everlasting. Instinctively, however, she knew what direction his thoughts were taking because hers were there, too.

''It hasn't changed at all,'' Dan remarked when Lynn had opened the door to her home and he had walked in and set his lone piece of luggage on the floor. ''Maybe an additional hanging basket or ceramic swan.''

''Did you really expect a major overhauling? It was only earlier this summer that you were here.''

''*Only?* It's been the longest time period I've ever spent in my life.''

Lynn chose to dismiss those words without a comment. As much as possible, she wanted to keep this meeting light and casual. Looking over her homey cabin, she sighed, ''It is beginning to look about as much like a shop in here as The Calico Cat does. I suppose I'm going to have to take the plunge and get some of this stuff back down there to sell. As you can see, I have this habit of going through the mechandise that comes in and not being able to part with some of it. After a while, it gets out of hand.''

"Don't apologize," Dan said. "I like your house. And I like you, Lynn Marsh. In fact, I more than like you."

"And that's why you made this mad, impetuous journey back to see me? I thought you were only using me as a stopgap and hitting me up for something cold to drink."

"As you well know, my purpose is *you*. But I am ready for something to soothe this dry, parched throat."

Lynn gave a quick, appraising look at his expensive suit, shirt, and tie. As hot and humid as it was, he must be sweltering.

"I'm assuming you have something more suited for this weather in that suitcase. Go on in the bathroom and freshen up. Feel free to shower if you want. Everything you need will be in there somewhere. In the meantime, I'll fix up something cooling and refreshing."

"And we'll talk?" he persisted.

"We'll talk."

When Dan had disappeared into the bedroom, Lynn washed her hands and splashed cold water on her face at the kitchen sink. She went into the bedroom and brushed the tangles out of her long, dark hair. Behind the closed door she could hear the streams of water from the shower hitting the tile walls. Looking back at the mirror over the dresser, she gazed at herself more closely than she generally did. She saw a young woman of twenty-five who appeared, perhaps, several years younger. The young woman wasn't bad looking with her shining hair, dark eyes, and a light summer tan that was more a gentle golden tan than a deep brown. In her blue and white sundress, she didn't look that different from girls seen in crowds and on busy streets in any town or city. Why? What was it about her that kept a prominent man who could have any woman he wanted coming to her when he had been told to stay away? Maybe it was just that. Daniel Resnick probably had never encountered a woman so determined to cut him out of her life.

Back in the kitchen, she arranged an assortment of deli meats and cheeses on one platter and filled another with olives, pickles, tomato slices, cucumber wedges, carrot sticks, and green pepper rings. By the time she had placed ice cubes in two enormous glasses and put them on the table along with a pitcher of tea, Dan had walked quietly into the room.

When she saw him standing there, wearing white tennis shorts and a navy polo shirt, his hair still damp from the shower and his eyes full of mute appeal, Lynn felt her heart turn completely over. In thinking back, she was never sure which of them made the first move. All she knew was that it felt marvelous to be held tightly in his arms and to feel the pressure of his kiss.

"I love you, Lynn," he said simply.

She nodded, then let her hands drop from his shoulders to the warm, smooth flesh just above his elbows for a moment before she moved completely away from him. "I've prepared nourishment for the weary traveler. I find it amazing that refreshments weren't served on your flight on the flying carpet."

"Oh, that genie of mine," Dan began with the lopsided grin she loved so well, "got all mixed up and booked me on economy class. First class you get a Persian carpet and harem girls who serve you mead and honey. I won't hold it against him. He is getting a bit senile but he meant well, and the important objective was accomplished: I'm here with you."

He sat down at the table of simple food, quickly downed a full glass of tea, and began to assemble a sandwich that would have put Dagwood's to shame for height. While he ate heartily, she sipped her tea and nibbled on the ham and pastrami.

"Aren't you hungry?" he asked. "I feel like a pig, eating like this while—"

"Don't worry," she interrupted. "I had a big lunch and it's really too hot to eat much. I usually have something light after dark when it's cooled down a bit, so just enjoy your sandwich and don't worry about it."

What she told him was true. The fact remained that, at that particular moment, she couldn't have forced down much food if she hadn't eaten a scrap for days. Her mind was too filled with turmoil about what she should do, what she should say, how she was going to handle this situation. The man said he loved her. She didn't doubt that he at least thought he did. He had the look of a man in love, and he had gone to all this trouble and expense despite her warnings.

Taking guarded looks at him as he sat across from her, she toyed with the idea of simply telling him the truth. Could she say, Look, Dan, you're already a United States senator with a lot of promise for attaining even higher office. And I'm the daughter of the former head of one of the biggest crime syndicates ever formed in Missouri. You'd have to give up everything to have me, because your political adversaries would immediately begin slinging mud and insinuating that you have syndicate ties. Even your friends and supporters would become wary of backing you for office, because a man touched by scandal isn't a good risk for the party. Even if they continued to believe in you as a man, they'd be worried the talk would hurt your chances.

He smiled at her gravely, took another bite of the gigantic sandwich, and chewed happily. Over the edge of it, his eyes held hers and spoke of tender things. No, it wouldn't work, she thought. Even though she hadn't been with him many times, she knew he was a determined man and, in a charming way, a stubborn man. He was also a warm, good man and would never coldly say, Well old girl, you're right. There's just too much liability connected with you. Thanks for being a good sport. Not Dan Resnick. She'd be willing to bet her life that he'd say, Don't be silly, honey, you're making a mountain out of a molehill. Most people forgot about Davy Marshall long ago, and no matter how hard they look, they'll never find anything to connect me with him—or with any other syndicate. I love you and you love me and that's all that need concern us.

Deep inside herself, she knew that with so much certainty that she realized she was going to have to be strong enough for both of them. And firm enough. Furthermore, she couldn't level with him. It just wouldn't work.

When he was through eating, he silently helped her put the things away. "Where shall we go to talk?" he asked.

"I thought you wanted to come here," Lynn replied.

"I did," he said, placing an arm around her shoulders. "I just meant should we stay in the kitchen, go to the front room, sit on the swing, or go down to the river."

"Let's take some cans of soda and go down to the river." she said impulsively. "Is that okay?"

"It's really what I wanted. Being sentimental, I keep remembering that's where we met."

She refused to meet his eyes and busied herself with the task of filling a small cooler with ice and a few cans of pop. She handed it to him, gathered up an old quilt, and called for Paddy. The three of them walked toward the winding river together, Paddy walking twice as far as they did because of all his futile side trips to chase rabbits and squirrels.

They spread the quilt in a smooth spot near the river. Lynn sat down on one side of it and Dan on the other. They were as far apart as the size of the quilt would allow. Dan opened the cooler, popped the top on one can and handed it to her, then opened one for himself.

"You wanted to talk, Dan," she said at last. "I'm not sure what to say. Nothing has changed. It never will. And I do so wish you hadn't come back."

"How can you say that? I see your face when you look at me. Unless I'm just a dolt so much in love he's seeing things that aren't there, you . . . well, you *care*."

"Of course I care. That isn't the problem. In fact, the caring only adds to the problem. If I didn't I could dismiss it all so much more easily. You refuse to accept my statement that there can be nothing between us. I refuse to give you the reasons for my statement. You're only prolonging the inevitable final parting, Dan. In the long run, that will be harder on us than making up our minds and getting it over with."

He took a long sip of the soda and sat the can down. "I thought all those things, Lynn. I kept away a long time, you have to admit that. I didn't call or write. Not even once. And I kept thinking it would get better. I even started seeing Diane McAllister more. We had dated from time to time, mostly at

63

political events because she comes from a very political family, but she began to show signs of getting serious, and my family and hers both thought that was a fine and dandy idea. My family and my advisers all tell me marriage would be good for my image. Great reason to marry, isn't it?''

''There could be worse. Tell me more about this Diane—what she's like, what she looks like.''

''She can't hold a candle to you,'' he said swiftly.

''I'm not fishing for compliments, Daniel. I was just curious.''

''Well, Diane's a great girl. She really is. She is attractive. One of those tall, leggy blondes who always manage to look as if they had stepped off the pages of a fashion magazine. And she's an ambitious young woman. Her father was Speaker of the House for many years. While she has no desire to be in politics directly, she still loves the life—the social occasions, fancy dinners, big charity balls, inaugural balls and parades. She'd like to be First Lady, and she sees me as a chance to achieve that goal.''

Lynn shook her head. ''I guess I just don't understand the political life. It all sounds a bit cold and calculating to me.''

He shrugged. ''She's not a bad sort. She has a sense of humor and is ambitious without being vicious about it. Diane's used to the life. She knows you can't be married to an active politician and have a stable, ordinary home life. We're really quite suited to each other.''

''Then why are you here?''

Dan's gray gaze swept over Lynn's features, and he didn't really have to use words to explain, although he did. ''I don't love her. There's a certain fondness, a certain affection. But she can go waltzing off on a jaunt with some other fellow and it doesn't bother me a bit. She does, however, want marriage. I was even on the brink of proposing until I ended up in this little corner of the wilds, trespassing onto your property. Until I met you, I was more or less convinced I'd never find the same quality of love Cara and I had. Now I know that isn't true. What I feel for you is special and it won't go away. I take Diane out, even hold her in my arms, and it's all so ridiculous. I don't want her.''

"And what about Diane?" Lynn asked softly. "Are you just assuming this is all cold and analytical with her because it is with you? Perhaps she loves you. Did you ever think about that? I have a feeling most women would, given half a chance."

He picked up the aluminum can, turned it in his hands, and regarded it as if it were a most interesting object. "I don't want to hurt her. I don't want to hurt anyone. She's a wonderful girl and deserves a good life. But I can't accurately assess the depth of any love she does or doesn't feel. Truly, as I said, she isn't a bad sort, but her feelings for other human beings seem to be rather shallow, superficial. And, again, I could be wrong. Maybe she's just a bit guarded because she's too proud to say anything until she knows exactly where she stands with me."

"And what would you do if you proposed—say, Listen, I'm not really in love with you, but it's about time I married and it's really the smart thing to do since we're so well suited? I can't imagine any woman feeling good about that."

"No?" He sighed deeply. "I'm not sure how I would word it. It's really immaterial because I won't be proposing. I have found the one I want and it's not Diane McAllister."

"But you date her, hold her, give her hope," Lynn insisted stubbornly. "You didn't, I thought, seem the type to be like that."

Dan reached out with a fingertip and touched her cheek lightly. "I have the feeling you've led a sheltered life, Lynn. It would be marvelous if people could be with each other as you think they should be. Truth is, however, that more people marry with an eye on what's in it for them than for love-sweet-love. That's just human nature. People turn their backs on lifelong friends to be chummy with someone who has more prestige or who is in a position to help them in some way."

Lynn was beginning to wonder if she knew the handsome man across from her as well as she thought she did. Maybe not. What she knew of him had been based more on intuition and perception that on intellect and experience. "Is that the way you see things, Dan? You didn't strike me as being that cynical. Somehow, when I look at you, I think of loyalty and friendship and loads of abstract virtues that to most people are words they hear but don't feel.''

He reached across the blanket and touched her hand lightly, letting it remain there. ''I didn't say I believed that that was the way people should do, my Lynn. And I didn't say I did that way. All I was telling you is that *most* people aren't bothered by what you refer to as the abstract virtues. I don't in any way feel I'm using Diane. I've never told her I loved her, and I've never insinuated that I want a permanent arrangement. And, where friendship is concerned, I've never knowingly hurt anyone or cut them out of my life for the sake of someone 'more important.' Sure, there are people I have to entertain and socialize with that I don't particularly care for personally. But I don't demean myself in the process, and I certainly don't inflict hurt on anyone I care for in order to make contracts or brownie points.''

Lynn swallowed hard and looked into his face. ''Somehow I get the impression I've just been chastised,'' she said meekly.

''Not really,'' he said with a laugh, giving her hand a firm squeeze. ''I just couldn't understand why you were so preoccupied with Diane when I'd already told you she meant nothing to me. And here we go again—I shouldn't have put it that way. She does matter to me. As a person and as a friend. But—''

''Run back to her, Daniel Resnick. Run back to her and say whatever you need to say to get her to marry you. From what you tell me, she's what you need. I can never help your career, can never be the wife you need. All I can ever do is hurt you.''

''How, sweetheart, can you be so sure of that? Right now, the way I feel, the worst hurt I could suffer would be to lose you. There's no way having you could hurt me. Not ever.''

Lynn felt like weeping, yet tears wouldn't help the situation. ''I feel like a broken record saying the same things over and over again. But it's necessary because you just aren't listening. Go away from me, Dan. Please, please.''

Instead of doing that, he cupped her face with his hands and gave her a long, sweet kiss. Lynn sighed, then indulged herself by responding to his kiss, letting her lips press against his and part under the pressure of his.

Slowly, like people moving in a slow-motion film, Dan pulled her into his arms and they rested full-length against each other on the faded pattern of the quilt. He murmured her name, nuzzled her neck lovingly, and let his fingers catch in the thick mass of her hair. It felt so good to be held, to rest her weary, lonely body against the strength of his, to know the peace and security of being surrounded by loving arms.

They lay there a long, long time, taking pleasure in tender caresses and in learning how to kiss each other in new and different ways. Lynn would grow breathless at the strong, demanding kisses that went on and on until her senses were reeling, then she would lie back, reach up to lock her hands behind his neck, and join with him in feather-light kisses and playful little nibbles on the lips.

"I love you, Lynn."

"It's really ridiculous, you know. Insane. Impossible. It really is."

"I know."

"I love you, too, Dan."

"And that's not ridiculous, insane, and impossible?"

"Of course it is. Even more so. Because I know why it can't be and you don't."

He held her tightly and she felt a slight shudder shake his large frame. "I don't intend to ask you any questions, Lynn. But I can't bear the thought of being without you. I just can't."

"Right now I can't bear it either. But—"

"Lynn, you said we could talk." His voice held a plea that went straight to her innermost soul.

"I know. And we can. We will. Right now, let's get back to the house before it's dark."

"What do you want me to do tonight? If you want to take me back into St. Clair to see if we can find a motel room for me, I won't be offended."

"I told you I trust you," she said with a smile.

"But I don't want to stay here if it will damage your reputation with anyone you know—with friends. Or . . . I never asked . . . for all I know, you might have a boyfriend of sorts."

"How little we really know about each other," she said softly as they gathered up their belongings and started back across the woods with Paddy staying close at their ankles. "There's no one at all to know or care what I do. No one. And especially not a boyfriend of sorts."

"You a hermit or something?"

"That's close," she admitted. "I can't be close to other people for the same reasons I can't get involved with you."

He gave a low whistle. "All the women in the world and I had to fall in love with a regular Madame X."

"Anyway," Lynn said, "it would be silly to drive all the way into town just to be told there are no vacancies. My mother's room hasn't been used since she died. You're perfectly welcome to it."

"It's close to yours?"

"Right next door."

"That's going to be great. To know you're so close I can call out your name and be heard. You don't know what hell I've been through, being such a distance away from you."

Back at the cabin, Lynn was quiet as she made up the bed in the spare room with crisp linens. When Dan kept insisting they had to talk, she pleaded that she was very tired and that they had all the next day.

As she lay in bed alone, she wondered if they would have been better off to complete the discussion and have it over with. She still didn't know what to do, what to say. Feeling like a small girl, she closed her eyes and said a silent prayer. She didn't ask to be able to have Dan, for she knew that wasn't possible. All she asked was the strength to handle the situation, giving Dan as little pain as possible. Tears trembled on her lashes and when she opened her eyes she defiantly blinked them back. Tomorrow was tomorrow and maybe the right words would come to her then. Strangely enough, she slept well. She hadn't expected to, but just knowing he was there and loved her . . . that was like being cradled in a warm cocoon. Sure, that cocoon was only temporary, but it was nice. So very nice.

Chapter Five

THE DAY DAWNED hot and sultry. With that sort of beginning, thought Lynn, there wasn't much chance for relief. For no particular reason, she thought about all the people who were camped out in the area. She felt a twinge of pity that their last long weekend before settling down for another autumn and winter of school and work had to be so miserably hot. Then she decided her pity was misplaced. The vacationers didn't *have* to be crowded along the river bank. They could be back in the cool, air-conditioned comfort of their homes. Any pity she had she should be using on herself. Here she was faced with the task of placing an ultimate rejection before the most desirable man in the world. Instead of pity, however, she felt quite optimistically cheerful—almost giddy.

She dressed quickly in bright yellow shorts and blouse and began rummaging about in the kitchen. This was going to be a proper meal, she decided firmly. On the occasions Dan had ended up eating at her house, she had served him cold food.

When Dan came to the doorway, apparently awakened by all of her clanging and banging, she looked up and immediately felt her heart go through its curious assortment of flip-flopping maneuvers that were the accustomed response to seeing him. He stood there yawning and stretching, wearing nothing but white tennis shorts. With his tousled hair and sleepy eyes, he looked for all the world like a little boy.

"I slept like the dead," he said after the yawns had subsided. "Must be the Ozarks mountain air. What *are* you doing?

You're making enough noise for a whole army of people."

"I'm cooking you a *real* breakfast," Lynn announced happily. "Eggs and little sausages and biscuits and gravy and pancakes with syrup."

He laughed at her. "All that? No wonder you're noisy. If we eat that assortment all at one time, we'll not be able to walk the rest of the day."

"You don't eat breakfast?" she asked hesitantly.

"Of course. I just don't generally have both biscuits and pancakes, but I'm sure it will be magnificent. Can you pause in all that a moment to give me a kiss?"

She did and would have felt content to remain in his arms forever if it hadn't been for burning the food. A few minutes later they sat across from each other eating, laughing, and talking until every bit of the meal was devoured.

"And you made fun of me," she accused when the last bit of pancake had slid down his throat. "You ate much more than I did."

"Well, after you went to all that trouble I didn't want to hurt your feelings."

"You did fine. I must confess, though, that there's a method to my madness. I stuff you now, and later, when the heat is unbearable, you won't have me cooking again."

Dan laughed again and helped her clear away the things from the table. "You're a very good cook, Lynn. You'll make some lucky man a great wife. May I place an application?"

His tone was light, but Lynn perceived that the words were edged with importance. "Let's finish up here and we'll talk about it," she replied. Her tone was as light as his, but she was careful not to face him.

When everything was terribly tidy and there was no way avoidance was possible, Lynn said in a very direct manner, "Okay, let's go have this talk you've come here to have." She led the way to the small living room and pointed out the couch to him. "You sit there and I'll sit here," she said, moving toward the maple rocker with the brightly patterned cushion.

"This doesn't seem to be the best arrangement in the world."

"I know," she agreed with a regretful sigh, "but if we sit any closer, that other business is likely to start up and the talking will stop."

"If you make that a promise, I'll come sit in the rocker, too."

"And we'd both end up on the floor. It wasn't meant to hold the likes of you. Now, are we going to be serious? Isn't that what this is all about?"

"I suppose so. But I would like to say that the chair definitely *was* meant to hold the likes of *you*. I can picture you sitting there, rocking our child. Our first baby. Dark-haired, I suppose; that would seem inevitable. I always thought Elizabeth was a pretty name for a girl. Of course, if you object, I'm not determined she *has* to be Elizabeth. And I'm willing to give you first choice on a boy's name. With the exception that I don't care for juniors and wouldn't like anything too fanciful. Such as Percival or Vladimir."

Lynn couldn't help smiling, although she knew she should be irritated at his stream of chatter, the only purpose of which was to delay her final edict.

"When do you have to go back, Dan?"

"Well, I can't stay until after the baby's born. I know that for sure."

Lynn broke out into an exasperated giggle. "You aren't playing fair, you know. To say you want to talk seriously, then acting like a talk show host or something."

"I'm sorry," he said most meekly, his twinkling eyes letting her know he wasn't sorry at all.

"Then, since you're so sorry, answer me: when are you going back?"

He lowered his eyes most humbly and replied, "If it isn't too much trouble, I thought you might drive me to the airport tomorrow? If you have more pressing things to do, I'll understand. According to all the rules of etiquette, I should be tarred and feathered. Not even Dear Abby approves of drop-in visitors. I considered this a unique situation, however, since I knew that if I told you I was coming, you would have immediately caught the bus to Wyoming or something. Which reminds me, have you ever been to Wyoming? I had it in mind for a honeymoon. A bit unconventional for such a purpose, but it has its advantages. There probably wouldn't be a lot of tourists in funny hats around.''

"Dan, Dan," she said, "what am I going to do with you? You talk as much as a thirteen-year-old girl. And make about as much sense.''

"Aren't you worried that you might hurt my feelings with such comparisons?'' he asked.

"Not in the least. As a politician, you must have buffalo hide where name-calling is concerned.''

"Ah, but it's different when it is from the lips of my sweet ladylove.''

Lynn did some quick thinking. If he was so determined to aim at levity, then she'd go right along with him. "Okay, then, let's be silly. We'll have fun today, tonight, and tomorrow while I drive you to the airport. I won't try to be serious even though I was suffering from the delusion that that was what you wanted. I won't try to make you see reason. We'll just enjoy each other's company. But you'll have to promise me one thing—''

"I don't think I'm going to like this.''

"You won't come back again without an invitation.''

"Okay,'' he agreed cheerfully and readily.

Lynn looked at him in surprise.

"You see,'' he explained, "the way I have it planned out, you'll ask me to come back. I plan to be so irresistible you'll be down on your knees begging.''

"Confident bloke, aren't you?''

"Only on the exterior. Inside I'm floundering around just like everyone else. I say all the things about marriage and babies

72

in a jesting manner, but it's what I want, Lynn. And when I want something, I don't give up easily."

What a perverse man, she thought. When she was trying to get him to be serious, he kept clowning around. Now that she had said they should just have fun, he started getting serious.

"You're an ambitious man, Dan. You've worked hard to get where you are. There's a lot of promise for the future. I couldn't be a very suitable wife for anyone. And especially not for you. To marry me would spell doom to your career in public life."

He looked at her with a strange gleam in his eyes, but he really didn't seem alarmed. "We're back to that, are we? And I don't even have to ask—you still won't tell what terrible things lurk in your past. Very well, then, we'll play a guessing game. You had illegitimate quintuplets when you were fourteen and put them up for adoption. You're a secret alcoholic. You had incestuous relations with your father who is an Albanian dwarf. You were a nun until you were kicked out of the nunnery for tippling too much wine. *You* were the one who originated the pyramid scheme. Tell me, am I close on any of those?"

Lynn shook her head slowly. "I won't say yea or nay to anything, senator. For if I do, you'll keep it up until you hit the right thing. If I were to agree to play a guessing game with you and play it fairly, then you wouldn't give up until you guessed it right."

"True enough. As in *Rumpelstiltskin*, there's always hope someone would slip me the right question to ask. Okay. I won't suggest such a thing again. But I will ask one question: *why* are you so determined not to tell me? Are you so afraid I'll hate you, be unable to forgive what you've done?"

He was so far off the mark that Lynn had to smile softly at him. It was a natural assumption that *she* had done something awful. She hadn't. So many of his jesting guesses about her past had to do with sexual escapades and here she sat across from him still a virgin at the age of twenty-five. "It isn't that at all, Dan. I think I know you well enough that, if I told my story,

73

you'd say, But it doesn't make any difference at all, my dear. But it does make a difference. If I let you persuade me it didn't, you just might end up hating me. When it was too late. When your political career had already been damaged beyond hope. It isn't easy to say good-bye. To me, though, it's infinitely easier to say it now than to watch your career die slowly by degrees . . . to regret that I hadn't been strong enough to hold out in the first place."

"Then you'll have to be strong enough for both of us, for I don't intend to give up trying."

"I will be," she said firmly.

"We'll see about that. We'll just see. Now, what shall we do today?"

"We could join everyone else and float down the river."

"Sounds fun in a way, but I don't relish the idea of sharing you with a lot of noisy strangers."

"I have an idea," she said with a laugh, then stood up suddenly. "Did you bring bathing trunks?"

He nodded.

"Ever been tubing?"

Dan grinned his endearingly crooked grin. "Not to my knowledge. Not when I was sober, anyway. And I haven't been otherwise since my college days. It isn't illegal, is it? Like gigging."

"Scarcely. Let's just go change. Then we'll pack up some snacks and go down to *my* part of the river, and I'll show you what tubing's all about."

He shrugged his broad shoulders diffidently. "I'm game for anything. Just so I get to be with you."

Lynn had him carry the picnic basket, and she carried the two rubber inner tubes. Dan looked at them suspiciously. "I think I'm beginning to get the idea. You mean for me to wear one of those things?"

"Not exactly."

When they got to the river and kicked off their shoes and put the picnic basket down after making sure Paddy couldn't get inside it to eat their refreshments, Lynn dropped both inner tubes in the water, then threw herself down across one and went floating off with the current.

"Hey, wait for me," he called. "How do you control this thing?" he asked.

"With great care. That's what makes it fun. Tubin', as they usually call it, is a great sport around here in the Ozarks. Inner tubes used to be the poor boy's canoe. Now they're really in."

Dan splashed about beside her, drifting along with the current. He still seemed a little skeptical. "But I really don't want to float all the way down the river and have to walk back. I assume we can't count on the current reversing and carrying us back to the same spot at our convenience?"

"You assume correctly, senator. The current isn't swift today. If it were, we couldn't do this. But the river is quiet enough that we can play around here for, oh, say a mile or less. We won't go out any farther to where the water is deeper."

"And so, I ask again, how do we control this?"

Lynn laughed at him and rolled off the inner tube, holding on to it with one hand and letting her feet touch the rock bottom of the river. "That's all there is to it. When you drift as far away from the bank—or as deep out into the river—as you want, you jump off. Or start swimming. All I ask is that you hold on to the tube. Irreplaceable items."

"I'm not worried about your idiotic tube as much as I am about my body. I can buy you a whole warehouse full of tubes if you insist. But, the way I understand it, this body is the only one I'm going to get a chance at."

"It's a rather nice one, though," she said agreeably, giving his well-developed body, bare except for black trunks, an appreciative appraisal.

"Hey, *I'm* supposed to hand out lines like those. Modern women. Bold, brazen hussies. And, I suppose, if I made a similar statement about your body, you'd hold it against me?"

"That's a corny joke, Dan. And a very old one."

"Does that mean you wouldn't hold it against me if I said you had a nice body, too?"

"That's exactly what I mean."

"Darn it. Whoops, watch it, I'm about to be swept away. What's that thing coming toward us? A crocodile?"

"More likely to be a dead tree limb. Crocodiles aren't found this far north."

"Is that because they read and obey your unfriendly NO TRESPASSING signs?"

"If so," she retorted, "that makes them more clever and/or law-abiding than certain legislators I could name."

They laughed and joked and played in the water, making frequent stops at the picnic basket for cold drinks and nibbles of cookies and potato chips. Paddy ran around and yapped at them but wouldn't come in the water. Dan told Lynn he thought Paddy was hurt because she hadn't brought him an inner tube.

"I guess we should go back," she suggested reluctantly when the sun was high overhead. "If we don't, we'll wrinkle up like a pair of prunes. And probably have dandy sunburns to boot."

"If we don't already," he replied, gingerly touching his own shoulder, which was a bit more pink than it should have been.

They slipped sandy feet back into their shoes and headed toward home with the empty basket and Lynn's inner tubes. Paddy's long, pink tongue was hanging out the side of his mouth, and he seemed most anxious to get home to the shade trees or to crawl under the house where it was cool away from the sun's hot rays.

Lynn took so much pleasure in the day that she didn't often stop to analyze it. When she did happen to consider the matter, she was amazed at the easy way she and Dan seemed to fit together. Getting to know him was exciting, of course. Yet, in a strange and profound way, it wasn't really getting to know him. It was more as if she had found someone she had once known well and lost. They had to fill in the gaps, but down where it counted, they already knew everything they needed to know. She loved and trusted him completely. She also liked him, respected him. With a sigh, she almost wished he could show a trace of meanness; then she could inflict herself on him. No way, she thought. And that was the irony of the situation: if he were less wonderful, she wouldn't feel badly at hurting him, but then she wouldn't feel the same quality of love and tenderness. So that was that. Her mind kept wanting to dredge up schemes, but the ominous fact remained: she couldn't have him.

That afternoon, Lynn and Dan made sure that every moment was occupied. Although neither of them said so, they both knew that it wouldn't be good just to sit quietly and talk. They dragged out a dusty croquet set and played several games in the blazing sun until they were both red-faced and sticky with perspiration. After that, they drank about a quart of lemonade each and sat inside where a breeze blew gently through the windows of the cabin and watched a very ancient—and very bad —movie. They made fun of it in such an extravagant way that they were helpless with giggles by the time it was over. Like the actors in the movie, they talked with fake British accents in a stilted manner.

When they got hungry, they lit the charcoal in the grill and hunted up a shabby Scrabble board and played a game until the coals were ready. They put the steaks on the grating and took turns playing chef. Once Lynn glanced up and caught such a dazzling look of happiness on Dan's face that she was almost blinded. Afraid that her own features were pulled into a similar expression, she reached toward him and hugged him about the middle while she buried her face against his shirt. That led to other things when he wouldn't let her face remain hidden, turning it up to his to cover it with kisses. While they lost themselves in the pleasure of touching each other, the meat nearly burnt.

"Love's grand," Dan said with a sigh as he regarded the

blackened steak dangling from the big fork, "if you don't care a lot for your stomach's feelings. For a stomach which is quite fond of medium rare, such an offering is an insult."

"At least we have the baked potatoes,"Lynn suggested helpfully. "No one can do much to a baked potato. Not even us."

However, by the time they had the rest of the food ready and the table set for the meal, they pulled the foil wrapped potatoes out of the coals to discover they were wrinkled and shriveled beyond belief.

"Burnt offerings,". Lynn observed while she scraped at the black surface of her steak. "Surely it's a sacrilege for mortals to eat burnt offerings?"

"Not when the mortals are hungry and the offerings were burnt for themselves. We didn't promise this food to some pagan idol, Lynn dear."

"It's just as well. Not even pagans would relish this. Aren't you glad, now, that I fixed you such a nice, healthy breakfast?"

"Of course, but that was absolutely hours ago. Really, this isn't bad once you get used to it."

He took a bite of the meat, and his teeth crunched against a charred bit of it. The incident threw them into an even giddier mood.

The food, bad though it was, managed to get consumed.

"We may," Lynn warned as they cleaned up, "bump into each other in the night while searching for the Alka-Seltzer."

"I can think of more terrible things," Dan said with a mock leer, "than bumping into you in the night."

"Food and sex. Do men ever think of anything else?"

Dan pretended to give the matter grave consideration. "Politics, automobiles, and sports. Those items have been given a bad name where male preoccupation is concerned."

"I suppose so. Care to tell me where your priorities are?"

"My, aren't we getting personal for a woman determined to keep secrets?"

"Forget I asked. You never tell the truth anyway."

He feigned hurt feelings and, making a funny face, remarked, "How can you talk to me like that? Don't you know I'm referred to as Honest Dan?"

"Oh, sure," Lynn said with a shrug of her shoulders, "but I thought that was one of those deals like where the fat man is nicknamed Slim and the tall one is nicknamed Shorty."

"No respect. You give me no respect at all. Red carpets have been rolled out for me at airports. Crowds of people have applauded me, given me standing ovations for brilliant speeches. And all you can do is insult me and make disparaging remarks."

"But you must love it. Why else did you come back?"

"For your famous charbroiled steaks," he said solemnly.

Lynn looked up at him and gave a happy little laugh. "Speaking of charbroiled, that's the way your nose looks."

"My nose?"

"Yes, your nose. It's quite black on the end."

She laughed again as Dan headed toward the mirror to look at himself. The dignified, handsome senator from Illinois. Sometimes she had to pinch herself to believe the man she had watched on television was the very same one who cavorted about in the water and made corny jokes and didn't seem to care if his nose were black or not. Instead of going to wash it off, he grabbed Lynn and pulled her to him. He then quickly proceeded to rub his nose against hers.

"Hey," she said, giggling and struggling in his arms in a way that wasn't serious about escape, "you're going to get me all dirty."

"So what? I want us to share everything, Lynn darling. What's mine is yours."

"That's great. Really great."

The frivolity was forgotten as their ardor deepened. Lynn ran her hands up his arms, feeling the soft warmth of the dark hair on his tanned skin. She murmured a sigh of contentment and pleasure as the firmness of his mouth increased against hers.

"You feel so good in my arms," he murmured. "So very

good. You've no idea how much I want you. No idea at all."

Judging from the combination of the fire raging within her own body and the close contact with Dan's, Lynn believed she had *some* idea about how he felt. For a long, luxurious moment, she gave herself up to the purely sensual tidal wave created by his nearness and deepening caresses. Then, with a firm move, she withdrew from his embrace. From the distance of only a few inches, she watched the wonder on his face and glowed inside at her ability to affect him so. Now that they were apart, a certain shyness seemed to hover between them. Lynn expected that from herself, but she certainly didn't expect it from the confident young senator from Illinois. With the slightly foolish expression he wore, the way his arms hung at his sides, and his hesitant manner, she somehow found herself wanting to ease the awkward moment.

"I think," she said, offering him a smile, "it's about time we played another round of croquet. Or maybe we can find the volleyball net in the garage somewhere."

He was able to laugh at her suggestion, and the laughter broke the tension in the atmosphere. "Is that why we've been having all these activities? To keep us out of trouble? I've gone along with everything you suggested, but I've had this feeling that you're acting like an activities director on a cruise or at a summer camp."

"Not really," she told him. "I think I've been more afraid of talking then I have of . . . uh, well . . . kissing and all that."

"Then if you're not afraid, come back," he offered, holding open his arms.

It took a great deal more willpower than she once would have thought to shake her head and retreat a few more inches. "That could only complicate things at this point, Dan."

"Did I ask for anything complicated?" he asked innocently. "Just another kiss or two. The others were so nice."

"Uh huh," Lynn agreed. "And getting nicer by the moment. Much too nice."

Dan didn't press the issue. Instead, he took her by the hand

and whistled for Paddy, and the three of them went on a quiet walk through the woods.

"I'll soak it all up," he said once, looking at the lush greenness all around them. "We'll walk awhile, go back to the house after dark. Then maybe we can sit on your porch and watch the stars pop out. Don't even feel obligated to talk to me, entertain me. Just knowing you're by my side is enough. Then, when I'm back in Washington, D.C., with all the business and harshness of my other world, I'll take out these memories: the feel of you in my arms, your hand inside mine as we walk, your lips parting beneath mine, the smell of pine and cedar and fresh, clean air, Paddy yapping and running as if he's accomplishing some great task. I'll remember all the white, gold, and purple flowers scattered about that are prettier than hothouse blossoms at thirty dollars a dozen, white clouds floating in a pale blue sky, the crunch of pine needles and leaves under my feet, the lap of the current against my skin while I floated in that crazy tube, our magnificent breakfast and burnt dinner . . ."

"You're going to remember *all* that?" she teased. "How can you plan on keeping your mind on how to vote and other important matters?"

He squeezed her hand affectionately as they moved along the path, weaving through the bushes and trees. "All that and more. As for important matters, I'll do the best I can. Know what, though?"

"What's that, hon?" she asked, rubbing her forehead lightly along the sleeve of his shirt, enjoying the chance to be with him, to touch him, to call him by endearments that came to her lips unbidden.

"To me, *this* is 'important matters.' If we could freeze time, have things like this forever, I'd stay here with you and never look back on what I'd given up. A man must be insane to think there are more important things than being with the woman he loves."

Lynn's heart stood still, then quietly turned over. How she loved him! If only she could have loved him a tiny bit less, she would have turned to him and said, Let's do that, then. Let's lock ourselves away here in this corner of the world and let the rest of it happen as it will. It has no bearing on us.

Instead of saying that, she smiled up at him and said, "But that isn't the way we're made. Not either of us. And especially not you. You couldn't give up your career if you wanted to. Not with a clear conscience."

"Test me," Dan remarked.

He said the words lightly, almost as if he were teasing, and Lynn responded by placing her free hand over his and exerting gentle pressure. Lynn was glad that the darkness hid her face, concealed the signs of the struggle between her mind and heart. She instinctively wanted to tell him the truth, to unleash the flood of pain and loneliness that had been rigidly contained inside her for so many years. By now, she knew beyond all doubt that she loved him, and she was just as certain of his feelings for her. But she was well aware of the ammunition the corruption in her past would give Dan's political adversaries. Knowing how very much it meant to him, she couldn't bear the thought of hurting—or ruining—his career.

"We'd better go back," Lynn suggested. "It will grow dark soon, and we don't want to be caught out here."

"Afraid of the bogeyman?" he teased.

"Maybe. Let's just say I have this thing about wanting to be able to see my enemies."

"When we get back to the cabin, will you sit with me on that rickety-looking swing on the porch and watch the stars come out, or will you absolutely insist on playing Scrabble and watching bad movies?"

"I'll watch the stars with you, though I must warn you that you might find it to be a dull experience. Stars don't really *do* all that much."

"I'm just in a funny mood, I guess, Lynn. I can picture us together on that swing, your head against my shoulder all sweet and trusting, your hair as dark and velvety as the sky, the little golden flecks in your eyes as bright as the stars . . . and that's what I want. Just to sit there with you. I have no plans beyond that moment. Crazy, huh?''

''Probably. But I like it. Especially the part where you compare my hair and eyes to the sky and the stars. You can say that again anytime you want.''

''Once is enough,'' he said firmly. ''I don't want a spoiled conceited woman on my hands.''

She didn't warn him that she wasn't going to be on his hands in any way after tomorrow. He already knew that. It couldn't hurt for them to have these last few hours without constant reminders.

A few moments later they settled down on the swing. They moved it gently, and the chains went back and forth with a comforting creaky sound. Paddy scampered about in the yard, did a bit of scratching, and finally settled down to chomp on a bone he had unearthed from its burial place. Twilight descended, then deepened. They didn't talk a lot, just a little nonsense about looking for the first star, then having so many come out at once that deciding which was first was impossible. Mostly they just listened to the night, to the katydids and birds that added to the nocturnal orchestration. The smells seemed to intensify as night fell, especially the heavy, sweet odor of the honeysuckle bushes near the house. In an effort to help out the stars, the fireflies sped around, flicking on their tiny lights. It was peace. Perfect peace.

The spell was broken only when they began to slap on their own arms and legs to fight away the mosquitoes.

''I think we're going to have to go in,'' Lynn suggested reluctantly, moving her head away from his shoulder.

''I know, but I don't want to. I want this to last forever.''

''But nothing does, Dan. And I believe the mosquitoes have us outnumbered in this battle.''

He gave a vigorous slap at his left arm, just barely missing the pesky insect that had landed there, and, with a sigh of acceptance, stood up.

They got cold drinks in the kitchen, then stood there in the harsh, artificial light, looking at each other and wondering how to go about the business of saying good night.

Dan cast a most beseeching look her way and once more held out his arms. Lynn moved to them swiftly, feeling as if she were going home after a long and busy day. Now she knew what to expect from his embrace. She knew how his arms felt about her, how their lips felt when pressed together, and that knowledge only increased her need for more.

"I love you, Lynn," he whispered softly, mouth brushing lightly along her temple and hairline.

"I know. And I love you, too."

His hands dropped to her waist, then after a few moments moved to enfold her hips. Lynn felt his deepening passion and responded. She returned his kisses with an artfulness and skill she hadn't known she possessed while the feelings churned and changed inside her. Never had she felt more alive and vibrant. Even her blood seemed to possess a will of its own, moving through her veins with the hot, heavy feeling of molten lava.

"Lynn," he murmured, and the way he said her name was a question in itself.

She wanted him. She wanted him as much as he wanted her. Perhaps more. Gently, sensuously, she moved her fingertips along the back of his neck, then downward to trace the line of the strongly muscled shoulders and back. Dan trembled slightly beneath even such a light touch, and she felt the soft shuddering of her own form as it molded itself against his.

His hands grew more bold and his mouth became quite demanding. How strong he felt to her touch, how good. But one of them was going to have to be in control of this situation, and Lynn, suddenly able to pull her face away from Dan's, knew she would have to be the one. He hadn't led her sheltered existence, and he knew what pleasures could be in store for them. Lynn could only imagine. In a way, that was part of her reason for breaking off this moment. Once Dan was aware of the fact that he was the first for her, Lynn felt that he would be even harder to convince that they should part, that he would somehow feel more responsibility toward her than he would have if she were an experienced woman of the world.

"I can't, Dan."

"You want to. I can see it in your eyes, feel your body tremble beneath my touch. If you can't give me forever, Lynn, I won't ask. But don't deny me this moment."

Emotions warred within her. When it came right down to the final commitment of making love with Dan, however, she just could not do it. Tempting though it was to steal a few moments of pleasure, she realized those moments could only complicate the inevitable outcome of this relationship . . . *and* make it that much harder to say the final farewells.

She shook her head and stepped a few more inches away from him. "If it helps the way you feel any, Dan, I don't think it's as much my virtue making this decision as it is fear. It's hard enough now to let you go. After we've been even closer, I might not be strong enough. So please try to understand."

"I don't understand. I don't at all. But I love you enough to believe in your sincerity. Good night, my love."

"Good night, Senator Resnick. You said you wanted memories to take out on dull evenings. Then add this: I love you and I always will. I love you so much that I want what's best for you in life and, sadly enough, that doesn't include me. Good night."

It was close to the time of dawning before Lynn's restless mind and body allowed her to sleep. Twice in the night she heard Dan moving around in the kitchen. She wanted to go to him. She wanted to so very badly, yet she lay there in the bed with her body held rigid. Her muscles were knots all up and down her spine and at the base of her neck. A hundred schemes ran through her mind. None of them were feasible. She couldn't have Dan Resnick. Her soft cotton gown was soaked with perspiration and clung damply to her body by the time she was so mentally and physically exhausted that sleep could no longer be denied.

When morning came, the little house was strangely quiet.

Even before she had left her bedroom, Lynn knew that Dan was gone.

A bouquet of wild flowers was on the table. He had gathered orange ones of a trumpet shape and tiny delicate-looking blossoms of periwinkle and white. She didn't know their names, but they were lovely. Gently, very gently, she touched the soft edges of the petals and bent toward the flowers to see what aroma they possessed. All the appraisal of the bouquet served to delay her reading of the note propped against the vase. Lynn looked up at the cabinet and saw that a fresh pot of coffee had been brewed. Feeling more than a little tearful, she poured herself a cup of the steaming brew and sat down at the table in the very lonely room. She took a few sips of the coffee, then unfolded the white piece of paper.

> My dearest Lynn,
> You didn't sleep last night. Neither did I. I suppose we've both said all we know how to say for the present. There isn't any point in making you drive me to the airport, then home again alone, after a restless night. I've arranged a way back home. For the moment, you're rid of me. But only for the moment. I'll never give up trying.
>
> Love always,
> Dan

She smiled slightly to herself and folded up the note to put away with her most precious sentimental possessions. He *would* give up trying. At the moment he didn't think so, but she knew he would. At heart he was a practical, ambitious man, and there was a limit to how much time and patience he would have for chasing elusive rainbows.

Lynn still wasn't sure if she was glad or regretful that he had returned to her this weekend. And it really didn't matter because what was over was over. She had a few more memories now to keep locked in her heart. Maybe, on cold, wintry days, those memories would provide a bit of warmth. She hoped so.

Chapter Six

THE SWELTERING HEAT finally broke. The red and white petunias that grew beside the little house in the wooded area blossomed brightly for a few days, revived from the high temperatures that had nearly killed them despite Lynn's early morning and late evening waterings. Going along with the spirit of things in general, the grass grew greener and thicker, and everything alive seemed to possess a bit more spirit. Even fat Paddy had resumed his pastime of chasing small woodland animals and snapping at passing insects instead of lying placidly in the yard pretending he didn't notice these offenders.

Lynn defiantly refused to submit to depression, nor did she allow herself to indulge in her prior practice of searching everything in the news media for word of Senator Daniel Resnick. She had told him—and herself—that there could be nothing else between them, so she forced herself to regard him as a chapter in her life that was over and done with. Dan didn't make achieving this objective exactly easy.

He had said he wouldn't come back until she asked him to. He had also said he wasn't giving up and planned to make himself irresistible. Lynn had expected a barrage of customary gifts and notes until he grew weary of the game. Flowers, candy, sentimental cards, silk scarves, bottles of cologne—those were the items she had expected to receive. Nothing of that sort arrived. Several times a week she heard from Dan, all right, but not in such a conventional way.

She received a bottle of vitamins with a scrawled note saying,

"Take good care of the body I love." One day an assortment of bulbs arrived with directions to plant them in the fall. "Long before they bloom, Lynn, we'll be together." A stuffed animal arrived—not a plush new one, but a woebegone bear with bald spots and a missing eye. "This is Herbie Bear, one of my oldest friends. As you can see, when I love something, I never let it go." The cards he sent were silly ones with crazy messages that made her laugh—not a rose or butterfly in the lot of them. He sent her packs of seeds to grow vegetables she'd never heard of, a red plastic Mickey Mouse watch "so you won't burn the steaks again," a cassette filled with every rendition of "Shenandoah" ever recorded, and a poster of the ugliest ape she had ever seen. Once she momentarily thought Dan had succumbed to conventionality when she opened a package and saw a glass bottle of perfume—a closer look and smell proved her wrong. The package had arrived via UPS at The Calico Cat, and Lynn had burst out laughing aloud to the curiosity of the customers and Margaret Johnson, the young matron who helped her out now and then on busy days during the school season.

"What is it?" Margaret asked.

Unable to reply for the laughter, Lynn held up the huge gaudy bottle which would have looked right at home in a flashy bordello. When she withdrew the stopper from the top of the bottle, the store was immediately suffused with the heavy, cheap scent.

"Are you going to try to sell *that* in here?" Margaret asked.

Lynn put the stopper back in as quickly as possible. "Oh, no, this is a gift from a friend."

"You're sure about that? I'd hate to see what he sends to an enemy. Take my advice, Lynn, and get rid of that admirer. Anyone with taste that bad must be a real dork, as the kids say these days."

"Actually," Lynn said, a smile softening her face, "he has marvelous taste. This is a joke. You should see some of the other things he's sent me."

"From the look on your face," the older woman retorted

wryly, "it wouldn't matter what he sent. He's definitely got a soft spot in your heart."

"Don't be silly, Margaret. It was just a little fling that's over. Nothing of any importance. It will pass." She briskly turned back to her work, but not before she saw the expression on her helper's face—a mixture of skepticism and pity. Was she that obvious, she wondered? Did everyone see her as a woman helplessly in love? Surely not. As she had told Margaret, it would pass.

As time went by, even the warmest of days turned chilly when the sun went down. Autumn was definitely on the way. It arrived on a dull evening that made the most valiant of flowers yield and crumple. The leaves began the process of turning from green to more brilliant colors and, finally, to crisp, dead brown. Lynn shifted the sundresses and sleeveless tops to the back of the closet and pushed the sweaters, knits, and woolly things to the front.

She placed the bottle of vitamins on the kitchen cabinet and took one each morning. It was probably a good idea, she decided, to take them. She didn't have a very big appetite anymore. Funny, but nothing tasted as good as that black steak and withered potato she and Dan had prepared together. Obediently, she planted the bulbs in a spot in the backyard. She put the vegetable seeds away in a drawer to wait for spring. She found Herbie a button that matched his remaining eye and sewed it on his careworn face. From scraps of fabric, she made him blue corduroy overalls and a red jacket with gold buttons down the front. When he was all bright and dapper, she sat him propped up against the lamp on her bedside table. She hung the ape poster on the inside of the closet door. All the silly cards and notes were put away with the note Dan had left behind Labor Day weekend. The bottle of perfume, ugly though it was, received a place of honor on her dresser. She was careful, however, not to open its top. Even the brief whiff she had released in the shop the day of its arrival had given her and Margaret headaches.

The funny, often corny, items kept arriving along with the notes and cards that alternated between the insane and the whimsical. Lynn found places for it all. She sent him nothing in return. If he received no response at all, he would stop. She was sure of that. A man like Dan Resnick—well, he didn't *need* her. Women would be easily come by for him, and some of them would probably be as persistent in their pursuit of him as he was in his of her. And one of these days one of them was going to be so pretty, so nice, so available, that all thoughts of Lynn Marsh would evaporate from his mind.

She hoped it worked that way. She truly did. Yet, along with that hope, she felt a certain sadness. What if . . . what if . . . that was a game the part of her that wanted to hope tried to play. She shut out thoughts of that dangerous game as much as possible.

Lynn well understood the importance of being safe, for she remembered what had happened when Davy Marshall had played dangerous games of his own. There really wasn't a way Lynn could reconcile her memories of Daddy with the portrait of a ruthless mobster who had been the cause of so much crime. Even, undoubtedly, of death. While she hated the hypocrisy, she still couldn't hate the laughing father who had adored, protected, and pampered her for seventeen years. She found herself being almost glad he had died when he had . . . before she had learned to hate him. That could have happened if she had spent years visiting him in prison . . . if he had confessed to her or attempted to justify his actions. She had been very young and vulnerable then, but now she was older and much stronger—and she was determined to fight the temptation posed by Daniel Resnick.

Soon all the trees were bare, branches reaching up toward a cold, gray sky to create a ghostly, barren look. To compensate for the outward gloom, Lynn put out the Christmas decorations in The Calico Cat and artfully arranged the new merchandise. Even before Halloween had come and gone, quite a few people started their Christmas shopping. Each time that Lynn sold a

Dawn Jarrel milk can to a customer, tears would cloud her vision and have to be blinked away.

The first snow came to the Ozarks, not a blizzard, just a gentle blanket of white that was gone in a day or two. As she had expected, the packages and cards arrived less frequently. She kept her self-made pact to not be such an avid newswatcher. However, like everyone else, she watched TV and read about current events with a fair degree of regularity. When she saw the black and white press photo of Dan attending a fund-raising dinner, she didn't look at it terribly long. She did look at it long enough to see the tall, poised blonde by his side. Perhaps Diane McAllister's perseverance was ready to be rewarded. That was as it should be. If Lynn couldn't have him, why should she hate someone else who could?

It wasn't in her to hate. Neither did her heart turn to cold, hard stone. While she wasn't exactly bitter, she was certainly lonely. The days and nights grew colder and colder. Mondays through Saturdays weren't so bad, not during the daytime hours. She kept busy. She didn't dwell on things. But the nights and those long, long Sundays. . . . Oh, God, she felt so alone.

Lynn knew that from January until early spring she could expect a lull in the store, but holiday shoppers kept her almost as busy as the tourist season had. She often had mail orders to fill. Of course, The Calico Cat wasn't so big that she put out catalogs and advertising brochures, but she would receive letters from faraway cities that would say, "I was in your shop last summer and have always regretted I didn't buy that lovely yellow and white quilt for my daughter. If you still have it, or a similar one, would you mind sending it to me? My Mastercard number is . . ."

"Look at this," Lynn said to Julie one frosty, busy Saturday. Julie and Kim were helping in the shop on weekends during the holiday season. "It's a letter from New York City. Some woman wants to buy six of those hand-blown vases. All in different colors. Six. Can you believe that? But only if I can get them to her before Christmas. That's only two weeks off.'

"Can you get them to her?" Julie asked with a grin, knowing the answer.

"At the profit I'll make off six of those babies? You bet I can. In fact, I'll go to the storeroom now and start finding all the padding I can for them so I'll have them ready for UPS Monday. I'll not complain, but it's hard for me to understand. She lives in New York City and orders things from *me*."

One day when it was slow, Lynn left Margaret in the shop alone and did her own Christmas shopping. It didn't take long at all. She had no one to buy for except the people who worked for her. She paused once and looked at the cashmere sweaters. Dan would look great, she thought, in one of those—the cream-colored, perhaps.

"Would you like to see one closer, dear?" the saleslady asked. "We'll monogram them without charge. They're selling very well. Just feel . . . so soft."

Lynn's fingers ran lightly along the sweater the friendly woman held out toward her. "Yes," she said softly, "it's very nice, but the problem is that I don't know anyone who could wear one."

The eager salesperson cast a quick look at Lynn's ringless fingers and said, "Oh, now, dear, a pretty girl like you must have a special boyfriend. Doesn't he wear sweaters?"

"I don't know," she replied vaguely, then walked away. And she didn't know. She had only known Dan in the summer. Even if he adored sweaters, she wouldn't dare send him one. Now that his ardor seemed to be on the wane, she couldn't risk stirring it up again. That wouldn't be good for either of them.

Christmas sales were better than usual. The shelves grew bare, and the nightly bank deposits were much larger than usual. Lynn helped fill the night hours by taking home her paperwork and planning her orders from there.

"Gee, I hope we have a white Christmas, don't you?" asked Kim, peering out the window of The Calico Cat on Christmas Eve.

"If that's what everyone wants," Lynn said. "I'd like it myself, but I feel selfish wishing because so many people travel to be with family and friends that it causes problems for them."

"So let them stay home," the young girl replied airily. "I want snow."

By the time they closed the shop, it was beginning to look as if Kim would have her heart's desire. The sky had that blank gray-white look that sets in when snow is forthcoming. By the time Lynn had the dark green Triumph parked snugly in her little garage, the first flakes were falling. She carried in the two bags of groceries and set them on the kitchen table. After changing quickly into jeans and an old shirt, she built a fire in the fireplace and made sure it was going strongly before she went to put the supplies away. She made a face at the frozen turkey roast in its aluminum pan. That, along with canned cranberry sauce and frozen dinner rolls, was going to be her holiday dinner.

For now, she opened a can of soup and went to sit in front of the fire while the soup was heating on the stove. Paddy sauntered across the room and curled up beside her, enjoying the warmth of the blaze and the feel of Lynn's hands scratching behind his ears. It wasn't long before the little dog was fast asleep. Lynn looked around her, thinking that the cabin didn't look like Christmas. She had used the excuse that she had taken all the decorations to the shop and had a tree there, so what was the point in decorating at home also? Who else would see it? It didn't matter. Christmas should happen in the heart, not just be holly branches and fir trees.

Her feet felt cold, and she slipped them into fuzzy blue slippers before she poured the hot soup into a big mug and curled up once more in front of the fire. While she ate the warming food, she watched the dancing flames of orange and blue. No, Christmas wasn't a matter of fir trees, homemade cookies, and cashmere sweaters. But it *was* a matter of sharing, of giving, of loving. I won't spend tomorrow like this, she told herself. She then began making plans. If the snow wasn't deep enough to prevent the drive, she would go into St. Clair and spend the day at the nursing home. She spent quite a bit of time there, not out of nobility but because she wanted to. Maybe even because it reminded her fully that there were people more lonely and forgotten than herself. It was an activity that kept self-pity at bay. Some of the elderly people she visited there didn't remember her from one time to the next, although they seemed to thoroughly enjoy talking to her when she was present. They liked to see her pretty face, they said, and took openhearted pleasure in the small gifts she brought. They talked of the past, remembering their early years in vivid detail, sometimes forgetting yesterday completely.

She was thinking of them, trying not to think about herself, and she was becoming sleepy, mesmerized by the licking tongues of fire within the hearth. Because she hadn't heard the car, she was completely startled by the knock on the door. A hope sprang up quickly in her heart, and she thrust it down immediately. It wasn't *right* to hope. It wasn't good. Besides, it had been two entire weeks since she had received a package or a note from Dan. But who else could it be? One of the girls from the shop with a last-minute gift or invitation. One of the neighbors who needed matches and didn't want to drive the several miles into St. Clair. Reluctantly she moved from her cozy nest to open the door and receive the cold blast of wind.

"Dan," she said, believing, yet not believing. She hadn't asked him to come and he had promised . . .

He stood there in an expensive topcoat. A Cadillac El Dorado in cream and bronze was parked just outside the door.

"I'm here," he said simply.

"So I see."

"Could I come in? It's awfully cold out here and it's snowing quite a lot."

She nodded slightly. He stomped away the excess of snow from his shoes and stepped inside. With a quick, impatient move, he shrugged off the heavy coat and hung it on the antique hat rack by the door.

94

"Hey, that's for hats," she said feebly.

"I don't have one."

She looked up at his black hair just in time to see the last of the white snow melt away. "You don't wear hats. Do you wear sweaters?"

He gave her a strange look and the corners of his mouth quirked into an almost-smile. "What do you think?"

Lynn burst out laughing at the sight of him in the corduroy pants and Fair Isle sweater. "I guess you do, at that. And a cream-colored one would have matched your car."

He walked across the room somewhat hesitantly, as if he were not quite sure she wouldn't throw him out into the snow. He asked for no explanation of her silly remarks about cream-colored sweaters. For a few minutes, he stood in front of the fireplace and held his hands out to warm. His back was toward her. His posture was tense and strained. Lynn wanted to laugh and cry at the same time. She wanted to run toward him and hold him to her. Instead, she stood back and waited until he turned around to face her.

"I try, Lynn, not to make promises I can't keep. In this case, I couldn't do it. I simply can't. It gets worse instead of better. Would you think I was exaggerating if I told you I've actually been suffering?"

She looked at his dear face, at the haunted look in his eyes, at the gauntness his cheeks hadn't possessed before. And he had lost weight. That was clear to see. His large frame was meant to carry more flesh than it carried now. No, she wouldn't think he was exaggerating. She could see that. He looked tired, seemed older than he had before, and that inner sparkle she loved so dearly was missing.

"What am I going to do with you, Dan?" she asked, her voice barely rising above a whisper.

"You could love me," he suggested, and he looked and sounded as meek as a very small child requesting a cookie.

She could love him, could she? When had it ever been otherwise? Love, real love, wasn't planned. It didn't happen as a matter of convenience between two parties who were well-suited and ready. As rain fell on the just and the unjust, so did love. It fell at random, and whoever happened to be there got the benefit—or the pain.

Lynn held out her arms and within a heart's beat, he was there. For quite some time they didn't kiss each other, or even move. They just stood there in the firelit room clinging to one another. He pulled away slightly and gray eyes looked deeply into brown ones. Love and desire raged separately, then suffused. Apparently Dan read all he needed to know in that look, for he scooped her up into his arms without an additional word and carried her toward the bedroom. At the doorway, he paused and kissed her lightly, then put her down.

She swallowed hard, unable to break away from the hypnotic quality of his slate-gray gaze. Maybe this moment, this event, had been inevitable from the first time they had met. All she knew was that she wouldn't be turning back. This acquiescence did not mean she was planning a future with him. It only meant this was going to be her parting gift to him—and to herself. To give to him the most precious gift a woman can give the man she loves. And after . . . well, right now she wouldn't think about after.

Kicking off the funny blue slippers, she sat down on the edge of the bed and held herself quite primly and stiffly. She looked up and at Dan to see him smiling at her in a most curious fashion.

"Is something wrong, Lynn?"

She shook her head as she bent to pull off the long knee socks that were a crazy combination of brown and pink. "I suppose I always thought my seduction would be accomplished with me in a lacy negligee and musky perfume, and here I am in fuzzy houseshoes and faded jeans and shirt."

"You're beautiful to me, sweetheart, in anything you wear. And what's the big deal about fancy nightwear? To accomplish things properly, it all has to come off anyway."

Lynn colored slightly, not sure exactly what she was supposed to do now. It was almost embarrassing to be so woefully ignorant at her age. She was quite sure, from Dan's manner, that he had no idea of the extent of her ignorance. Except for a physician occasionally consulted, no man had ever viewed Lynn's naked body, let alone touched it intimately.

She stood up slowly and took off the bedspread, then turned down the blankets and top sheet to reveal the snowy linens and pillows beneath. Dan's eyes followed her through every movement, then strayed to examine the contents of the room.

When he spoke, his voice sounded choked. "All that time you wouldn't break down and write or send me a token of any sort. There were times when I actually doubted that you cared anything about me. But you do care, don't you?" Without giving her a chance to answer, he continued, "You've kept everything I sent. I see Herbie and that gosh-awful bottle of perfume and even that crazy Mickey Mouse watch. It's all just junk, really. You would have thrown it out immediately if you didn't love me."

"You're calling Herbie Bear junk?" she asked, picking up the stuffed bear and turning him over gently in her hands.

"He's not to me. It was possible you'd think so."

She shook her head. "I was very touched. And I do love you. You should know that. I always have. I've just tried to be wise and strong, Dan."

"And now?"

Looking at him directly, her eyes didn't waver. "I guess I'm tired of being wise and strong. What do we do now?"

He laughed heartily, and the sound caused a strange prickling sensation all over her body. "We make love, I think. Unless you've changed your mind."

"It isn't that. I was just wondering if I should go to the bathroom and put on my nightgown, then slip into the bed and pull the cover up to my neck while *you* go into the bathroom and put on your pajamas."

"Pajamas?" he asked with a lift of his eyebrows. "I didn't bring any. And as for nightgowns and covers up to your neck, well . . . all of that is as unnecessary as my pajamas. Come here.''

Lynn obediently walked into his open arms and felt his lips travel tenderly across her face and neck. He took his time, kissing her gently until her ardor matched his own. For a moment, Lynn allowed her sensations to float, but as his caresses grew bolder, she became fearful.

"Dan?" she asked, pulling away from him slightly.

"Yes, love?"

"Please be patient with me. Show me what you need for me to do."

He was suddenly quiet. "What are you telling me? That you've never done this?"

"Not ever."

When he looked down at her in apparent disbelief, she added quickly, "But I'm sure I'll learn fast if you'll only be a little patient. I wouldn't have told you, but I've read that it can sometimes hurt the first time, and I wouldn't want you to hurt me, because you'd worry about it, so I decided perhaps I should tell you. Do you mind terribly?"

He continued to look at her without words, so she kept on talking nervously. "Or would you rather I hadn't told you? Perhaps it won't be difficult, and then you'd never have known. Oh well, I guess you'd know even if it didn't hurt me, because I won't know the proper things to do."

"You're talking too much," he said tenderly. "That's my department. Just relax. Do what comes naturally, do what feels good. It isn't difficult at all, and I'll try very hard not to hurt you."

The talking and explanations had created a nervousness that took the edge off her desire. With great tenderness Dan rekindled that desire until her body and soul were his and his alone.

"I love you, Daniel Resnick," she said, running her lips and tongue along his shoulder, loving the damp saltiness that was the aftermath of lovemaking.

"I love you, too," he said with a laugh, "but you should have told me long ago about . . . er, your maiden state. In this day and age, a man doesn't really expect to find . . ."

"Do you mind?" she asked anxiously.

"That I'm the first for you? *Mind*? Far from it. You, in every way, are the most fantastic thing that's ever entered my life."

"I feel the same way about you." She gave a luxurious sigh and rolled over so that she could view him in the dim light. "Actually, if I had known how fine and *easy* this all was, I might have started it up years and years ago."

She was only kidding, but she didn't want to get too serious at the moment. Lynn didn't want to be praised for virtue and strength, because she herself had no way of knowing how much of her holding out was due to those factors—and how much to the fact that she couldn't allow closeness.

"That's another reason," Dan said lightly, nuzzling his mouth in the hollow of her throat, then running his tongue along her earlobe, "that I'm glad I'm the first. Because if I make you feel good at all, you'll think I'm fantastic since you have no basis for comparison. But being your first isn't nearly as important to me as being your last. You know that, don't you?"

First, last, only. She looked into his eyes and nodded gravely.

Outside, the snow continued to fall. Lynn couldn't sleep. When she thought Dan had dozed off, she got up, wrapped a robe around herself, and threw some more wood on the fire. Then she went into the kitchen and washed the few dishes from her small meal.

He joined her in the kitchen, and she was about to express her surprise when she noticed the blanket wrapped around him.

"Are you having a modesty attack?" she asked, laughing.

"No, but my luggage is still out in the car, and it was cold in that blasted bedroom without you there to warm me. Could we maybe cuddle up in front of that roaring fire?"

"Sounds like an excellent idea. Hungry?"

"Not really. I just want you."

Lynn smiled at him and gathered up a couple of quilts and some pillows. Dan helped her improvise a bed on the carpet in front of the fireplace.

"I like this," he announced when they were stretched out together. "All I have to do now is take off that robe and watch your lovely body in the firelight."

"Is that all you're going to do?" she asked teasingly. "Just watch?"

"Probably not. Since I have such an eager and apt pupil, I'll probably give you another lesson in eroticism. How does that sound?"

She enjoyed his next lesson thoroughly. Apparently he did also, for Dan announced that she had earned an A+ and was now ready for the next plane in higher learning in the area of lovemaking.

They slept nestled there together before the fire. When morning came, they ate a light breakfast, made love again, then showered together before they dressed. The frozen turkey and rolls suddenly became much more festive now that she had Dan to share them with her.

"Merry Christmas," he said shyly, holding up a gaily wrapped package.

Lynn hesitated, feeling embarrassed because she had nothing for him, and ended up telling him about the cashmere sweater she had wanted to buy and didn't.

"Don't worry about it, Lynn. You couldn't have known I'd break my promise and come here to you. Now open the silly present."

And it was a silly present. He had gift wrapped a pair of padlocks. When she asked, "Whatever are they for?" he replied, "They're to double-lock your car with when you have the convertible top down."

She made a face at him and threw the red and green ribbon around his neck. Then, nestled in the cotton underneath the brass padlocks, she found the ring. It fit her finger, and it had the biggest diamond she had ever seen. "Dan," she said breathlessly.

"Don't say no," he told her quickly. "In fact, don't say anything at all. Just keep it for a while. I have to leave tomorrow. It's unavoidable. But this is Christmas Day, so don't go throwing it back in my face immediately. Think it over. Just for this one day, whatever you decided after, it will give me pleasure to see you wear it."

After they had eaten their funny and festive Christmas dinner, Lynn asked Dan what he would be doing if he hadn't come here.

"I'd be at my parents' home surrounded by brothers and sisters, nieces and nephews, aunts and uncles and cousins. There are so many of them they'll scarcely notice I'm gone."

"But you did tell them, didn't you?"

"I told them I was coming to have one more shot at winning the woman I love. They tactfully asked no more questions. You'll like my family, Lynn. They're great people."

"I don't doubt that," she replied, touching the lovely crinkles at the edges of his eyes. "If they produced you, they'd have to be."

"And what were your plans for the day, Lynn? To stay here all alone?"

Feeling slightly embarrassed, she told him what she had planned to do.

Impulsively, he said, "We still can. We have the whole afternoon. I'd love to spend every minute of it with you, but it's Christmas Day and that's no time to be selfish."

"You mean it, you'll go with me?"

"Of course."

Lynn changed clothes and gathered up a number of small articles, candies, cigarettes, talcum powder, magazines—the little extras that elderly people in nursing homes often don't have.

Needless to say, Senator Resnick had the little nursing home turned upside down before they left. They certainly hadn't been prepared for such a prestigious visitor . . . and with no warning at all. He laughed and joked with the personnel. He shook hands with the elderly men and women and listened to their opinions—often quite outspoken ones—on political matters.

"Now I know why you're a success in politics," Lynn said wryly as they climbed the winding road home in the El Dorado. "It should be illegal for one man to possess that much charisma."

"Nonsense. And anyway, this charisma won't do me much good if it won't win you for me. How about it, Lynn? Are you ready to give up the stubborn game?"

It was at that moment Lynn made her decision. She knew what she had to do. Reaching out, she touched his hand, which rested lightly on the steering wheel. "I love you very much," was all she said.

At Dan's suggestion, the evening meal consisted of frankfurters roasted over the fire in the fireplace. After the food was eaten, they let the fire die down and headed for Lynn's bedroom. She moved eagerly into his arms, and the night was filled with magnificence and pleasure.

"I don't want to leave you," he said when morning came, "but I absolutely have to. I hope from now on you won't be so eager to get rid of me. Oh, how I love you, my Lynn."

"I love you, too, Dan," she replied softly, lifting her face for his farewell kiss.

"I'll be back soon. And, before that, I'll call and write. Nothing can keep us apart now. We're really and truly one. You have to marry me to make an honest man of me. We can't have a senator with compromised virtue who's always running off to the wilds and woods to make love."

She laughed at his foolishness until the door was shut and she heard the Cadillac drive away. Silence descended over the cabin and her laughter turned to sobs that racked her slender body.

Chapter Seven

"YOU'RE SURE THIS is what you want to do, Ms. Marsh?"

Lynn looked across the polished desk at Jeffrey Bain, the young attorney who had recently opened his office in the rooms above the hardware store in St. Clair.

"Yes, I'm sure," she replied evenly.

He shrugged his shoulders and moved about in his chair as if he were uncomfortable. Lynn was beginning to wonder if she should have chosen an older, more established representative for her legal business. Perhaps her unusual state of affairs wouldn't have made a world-weary attorney quite so nervous.

"It's a bit unorthodox. That's why I asked, just to be sure. It isn't every day that one encounters people who want to disappear. Not in St. Clair, anyway."

"You'll know how to contact me," she said with a smile so dazzling it was calculated to take his mind off all else. "As I've said, it's important that you keep this information confidential. If I could afford to do so, I'd simply walk off and leave my shop and property, but I can't do that."

"And it wouldn't be a terribly responsible way to behave," he replied, giving her a very censorious look that made her want to laugh. She could tell he was taking *his* responsibility as a counselor seriously and wasn't about to yield to the lure of appearing human. Oddly enough, this attempt at stern, authoritarian behavior made him seem more immature than he probably was—like someone with a baby face growing a moustache and wearing a hat.

"That's true," Lynn agreed. And it was. She loved both The Calico Cat and her cabin in the woods too much to lock them up and leave them to decay or be vandalized. This way, Jeffrey Bain would have the cabin and land in the hands of a real estate agent. For a small fee, he would have the property seen to until it was sold. He was also taking care of the legalities of transferring ownership of The Calico Cat to young Julie's parents. When she had told her employees she was leaving but that they could work in the store and keep it open until it sold, Julie's father had contacted her later that evening. His wife was all excited, had always dreamed of running and owning her own business, and knew that The Calico Cat was well-established.

Lynn hadn't expected it to be that easy. If only she could sell the house as quickly, but she supposed that was too much to hope for. Her plans were rather nebulous. All she knew was that she was going to move on. Until she found a place she liked, she would rent a small apartment and work as a waitress or something . . . some type of work that didn't demand permanence or commitment.

"And you want to sell the house furnished?" asked Mr. Bain.

Lynn nodded, thinking of the furniture she had bought and fixed up over the past several years, of all the refinishing work she had done on the antique items. She thought especially of the wooden rocker with the bright cushion she had made for it. As much as she had loved all these things, they were, when all was said and done, only things. It would be infinitely simpler to move without a lot of possessions or worrying about storage fees or being traced through moving companies or moving vehicle rental companies.

When the lawyer was sure he knew what she wanted, Lynn asked what she owed him for the present. He was still new enough to be embarrassed at charging people high fees for what seemed like only talking to them. When he named the sum, Lynn wrote out a check and handed it to him with a good deal of outward composure. Inside she was shaking like a leaf.

"Cash that soon, Mr. Bain," she advised. "I'll be going to the bank by the end of the week to close out my accounts. They would like all outstanding checks presented by that time if possible."

He nodded, knowing he never delayed in cashing checks. His eyes followed the attractive woman to the door. He didn't try to hide his curiosity, but he did refrain from asking questions. It was his suspicion that she wouldn't have answered them anyway.

Lynn knew that the people who had worked for her were curious about where she was going, and she was grateful that they didn't press her for answers. She didn't want to tell any lies, and she wasn't sure she even knew the truth.

One of the hardest things she had to do was leave Paddy at the home of Margaret Johnson. After a great deal of painful deliberation, she had decided that there was no way she could take the little dog with her. Lynn was certain that Margaret would take excellent care of him, but a painful lump formed in her throat as she told her about Paddy's favorite foods and his fondness for bounding after squirrels in the woods. Lynn would never forget the sight of him chasing her car for the last time as she pulled out of Margaret's driveway.

The Triumph was so small that it took Lynn several trips from the cabin to The Calico Cat to deliver all the antiques and decorative items that she had included in the inventory she had sold to Julie's parents. And, of course, she thought, the Triumph was another liability. Wasn't she going to be allowed to retain any part of the old life she had come to love? She ran a hand over the dark green fender and pondered the situation. Perhaps she could risk keeping it for a while. It was a good car, with low mileage, and very economical to operate. Since she didn't plan on changing her name again, it would probably be possible for Dan to trace her anyway. What she had to do was make sure he wouldn't want to trace her.

She packed as much of her clothing and personal items as the car would carry. The remainder she put in packages and addressed them to herself at the small town in Arkansas she had picked out at random while looking at the road map. Not wanting to have to swear the post office employees to secrecy, Lynn didn't give them her forwarding address. Instead she left careful instructions to forward her mail to the office of Jeffrey Bain. These instructions caused a few raised eyebrows, but raised eyebrows didn't bother Lynn as much as a lot of other things. Her main regret was in the pain she was causing Dan. She should have been wiser and smarter, should have found some way to discourage him before they had become so deeply involved. *If* she hadn't accepted his invitation for the fish fry . . . *if* she hadn't responded so eagerly to his embrace . . . *if* she hadn't let her heart beat so rapidly when he merely walked into sight. All the ifs didn't matter now.

The cabin was locked and its keys were in the possession of Jeffrey Bain. The keys and bookkeeping work of The Calico Cat had already been turned over to Julie's parents. Her out-of-season clothing would probably arrive in Arkansas before she did. The bank had been instructed carefully in the handling of her funds, and a notarized letter gave authority to Mr. Bain for the transacting of her business. Some would say it was a mistake to place so much trust in a young man she didn't really know. He could easily work out something to make it appear that he sold her property for less than he did. Lynn didn't believe he would do that. And she had to trust *someone*. Before taking off on the highway in the little green car, her last act was to push a first-class letter into the slot at the St. Clair post office that said OUT OF TOWN MAIL.

Dear Dan,

I know I'm taking the coward's way out, but it would be impossible for you to understand if I were to tell you this face to face. I can't settle down with you. There are no mysterious reasons as I once pretended. Some people are simply dreamers and drifters by nature and are incapable of meeting the demands of permanent relationships and commitments. Well, I'm one of those people. Believe me, I know myself well, and I just don't have any depth to my feelings. That's why I shy away from relationships of any sort. Everyone seems to expect or need some type of love and loyalty I just can't give. I don't want to hurt anyone, but I know my emotions are like driftwood. When I wake up each morning, I never know what I'll feel or want. What we had together was nice. It provided some warmth and laughter. That's all. I could see you wanted it to be more than that, so I've just drifted on. It would have happened soon anyway. The soles of my feet were getting itchy.

Take care,
Lynn

As she drove south, Lynn decided that writing those words was the most difficult thing she had ever done. Facing her father after his arrest had been hard, but he had deserved his punishment. Burying her mother had been hard, but she knew Mother had really wanted to die. Losing the people she had thought were friends when the trouble with her father hit had been hard, but not *this* hard. Daniel Resnick had done her no harm. All he had done was love her and turn his trust completely over to her. Nothing she had ever been able to say had dissuaded him from loving her, from pursuing her. Moving away wouldn't dissuade him now if she had said the same old words, "I love you but it just can't be." Telling him that she didn't take him seriously enough to marry him and make a life with him was the only thing that would keep him from trying to trace her and bring her back to him.

Thinking of that hateful letter made tears come to her eyes. Soon they were flowing freely enough that her vision was obscured, and she pulled off onto the shoulder of the road, pressed her forehead against the steering wheel, and let the tears have their way. After a while, she grew quiet, and became aware of a tapping sound. Alarmed, she looked up, afraid that she might see someone with a gun or a threatening look. She saw a highway patrolman, tall and handsome in his blue and black uniform and broad-brimmed hat. He removed sunglasses to look at her with eyes filled with grave concern.

"Are you all right, miss?"

"I'm fine," she said, turning a tearful face to him that didn't look fine at all.

"I didn't want to scare you, but it didn't seem right just to pass on by with this little car parked here. It's really a dangerous place to park. Someone could come around that curve at a high speed and knock you down into that valley. Better move on," he said kindly.

"I will. Right now. Thanks for stopping."

He twirled the dark glasses around in his hand and seemed hesitant about walking away. "You sure there's nothing I can do, sure there's no problem with the car?"

"Yes, I'm sure. I'm afraid I've just been a bit silly. I split up with my boyfriend and went on a crying jag I wasn't expecting to have right in the middle of the highway. I feel better now."

"That's fine," he said awkwardly. "Nothing like a good cry to make a person feel better."

"Sure thing," she replied, with an attempt at a bright smile. "Thanks again for stopping. I'll move on out ahead of you if it will make you feel better."

"Please do," the officer said, seeming relieved.

Lynn nodded, turned the key, and eased the sports car onto the black-topped surface. When, after a few miles, the trooper turned off to complete his round of duties, he gave her a jaunty wave and she responded in kind.

Radley, Arkansas, population 3,722, was somewhere down the road. It was an odd sort of place for a girl from the exclusive urban Frontenac neighborhood of St. Louis County to pick. No one would ever dream of looking for her there. No one at all.

She spent the night at a small motel near the Missouri-Arkansas border. The next day she pulled off the highway onto the access road that led to Radley. The town seemed to have only two motels. Neither of them looked very appealing. Radley didn't have the asset of being a vacation spot. High-priced accommodations weren't much in demand here. Even though Lynn told herself she didn't care what anyone thought, her cheeks burnt high with color when the motel clerk gave her a knowing leer as he handed her the keys to her room. She couldn't really blame him for his attitude.

She was a young, good-looking woman with an expensive coat and a sporty car—and she was checking into a motel in broad daylight on a frosty day at the end of December. Lynn knew what he was thinking: that her lover would be meeting her soon. She wondered if the clerk had her pictured as a call girl or as a woman meeting a married man. She did not, of course, care enough to ask. Somehow she felt the beady-eyed man would be disappointed in the way she spent the next few days and nights until she found a better place to live.

When she unlocked the door to the motel room, she shuddered slightly. If she were going to stay in Radley, it wouldn't take her long to find a better place. It was obviously a cheap, sleazy room meant for the hasty consummation of cheap, sleazy affairs. The sights later in the day, after she had rested awhile, weren't a lot more cheering. Radley didn't have the picturesque quality St. Clair had possessed. She wasn't too keen on settling there, but decided she should stay at least a few weeks before confusing Jeffrey Bain more by moving on so quickly.

By the time darkness had crept over the sky, she had found a clean though shabby apartment above a grocery store. It wasn't a palace, but it was definitely more acceptable than the motel. The present tenants would be out by the first of the week, and Lynn could transfer her belongings then. She also found the promise of a job. Her wages as a waitress would be small, but the owner of the restaurant seemed kind, and Lynn could tell he was hoping that she would bring in business—that the local residents would drop by to see the new woman who had drifted into town and would stay for a sandwich or plate lunch.

It worked. At the end of two days, the balding proprietor of

Chubb's Diner looked at Lynn and shook his head. "You're too classy for this place, lady, but as long as you bring in business, I won't ask questions."

Lynn paused in her action of clearing off a corner table and glanced over at him. "It won't last, you know. It's a small town. Soon they will all have seen me and they'll know I'm not for hire and will grow tired of watching me and my dull life."

He looked her up and down, eyes flicking over the neat black slacks and white blouse. "You underestimate yourself, Lynn. And other people. It's good to look at a woman like you even when you know that's all you can do. Besides, you're a damned good waitress. Polite. Never mix up orders. Well, not much, anyway. Customers like the way you treat them, like they're special."

Lynn felt embarrassed—and somehow touched. After mumbling a thank-you, she turned swiftly back to her work. How odd life was, what twists and turns it took. Once she had been an honors student at a prestigious private school. Even under the assumed name, she had completed her education and graduated near the top of her class from the Sorbonne. She was fluent in German and French and could get by in two or three other languages. Once she would have spent on a single garment more than she could make here in a year's time. And yet she felt a glow of praise at being called "a damned good waitress." It was really pathetic, she thought, to need a bit of human kindness that badly.

She couldn't stay in Radley. She just couldn't. For the present, she would make do. But by spring, she would move on. Perhaps Jeffrey Bain would have sold her house by then and she would be free to find a better place to live. Radley and everything about it was too squalid to be endured permanently. Maybe she would buy into another small business. Or, if she wished to use her education, maybe she would go back to Paris. She could get a more-or-less permanent visa, take a teaching job. Questions wouldn't be asked there as much as in the

United States. Over there, they could care less about Davy Marshall and her possible connection with his shady world.

The days passed. She made many tentative plans but no concrete ones. She tried not to think about Daniel Resnick, but that proved to be impossible. Even on days when she worked double shifts in the funny little diner, he was never off her mind. The place could be crowded with people vying for attention, in haste to place their orders, and she could keep on the run until her feet were aching and swollen—yet Dan was always there, just a part of her. At any given moment she could hear his voice, see his face, feel the taste and pressure of his lips on hers.

All the crazy things Dan had mailed to her during the autumn were present in the new upstairs apartment. Even the vegetable seeds. Where she might be in the spring that she could plant rutabaga was uncertain, but she kept the seeds all the same. She wondered if the bulbs she had planted at the cabin in St. Clair would come up this spring—or if they would not bloom until the next. Herbie Bear sat on the bed by day and occupied the other pillow at night. She would look at the worn stuffed animal and imagine Dan as a little boy and how he must have looked holding the bear. Then she would imagine another little boy holding Herbie . . . a small boy who looked a lot like Dan and a little like her. At such imaginings, she felt a pain not unlike a knife twisting and turning within her heart. In her mind, she knew such things could never be, but somehow her heart and soul could not stop wanting, hoping. But it was all fantasy, for Lynn was well aware that she would never be the mother of Dan Resnick's child. The moon was more attainable to her.

Winter deepened and was dismal. January and February were both bitterly cold, with frequent snowfalls. Compared to locating a new place to live in subzero temperatures on icy highways, Lynn found that staying in Radley was bearable. That didn't mean she had decided it was a vitally cheery place, but when she kept telling herself it was only temporary it didn't seem so bad.

The upstairs apartment wasn't exactly a penthouse. It was, however, warm and comfortable. When she had to work nights and sleep days, she didn't even mind the constant noise from the store below. It was somehow comforting to know people were bustling around close by, and their clatter and chatter provided a lull that enabled her to relax far more than total silence would have. Her boss at the restaurant had been right—business didn't slack off. Burly, roughly dressed men continued to eat their meals there. They smiled at Lynn shyly in a schoolboy way over the rims of their coffee cups and gazed at her with adoring eyes when they thought she wasn't looking.

Lynn had thought she might move on in March. She spent a lot of time looking at road maps and travel brochures in her apartment. When March came, though, it didn't bring any hint of spring. Instead, another several inches of snow fell during one night in early March and covered the dirty, gray stuff that had never melted from the previous near-blizzard.

She went to work as usual, walking because she knew the snow was too deep for the Triumph Spitfire. The car was so low to the ground that if it slipped off into a drift, it would be stuck until spring—or until she hired a tow truck. The only customers who ventured out to eat at Chubb's were the truck drivers and construction workers who would perish before they'd let adverse weather conditions keep them home. The atmosphere wasn't very lively. Only four tables were occupied, and the men who sat at them were more inclined to chew their food slowly and stare at the television set behind the counter than they were to banter and laugh as they generally did. Lynn watched the hands of the clock. Never had they moved more slowly. It was ten o'clock in the evening, and she had two entire hours to go. She was already debating the wisdom of walking home at such an hour, but in Radley there was not much alternative. From what she knew of them, the two people who drove taxis weren't about to get out of bed in such weather to drive her a mile or so.

"We interrupt our regularly scheduled broadcast to bring

you this special news bulletin. Authorities have released additional information concerning the shooting incident in Washington, D.C., earlier today. Spokesmen state that a gunman managed to elude Secret Service agents and enter the Sheraton Hotel where the President was delivering a speech and was the apparent intended target of the gunman, whose identity has not yet been released although he has been apprehended and is in custody under heavy guard.''

"Ain't that sumpin'?" remarked one of the men at the corner table. "There's always some crazy runnin' around with a gun tryin' to make a name for hisself.''

"Now this'll make the bleedin' hearts go yelpin' for gun control again," remarked his companion.

"Boy, that's the truth, Jim. Sad thing is, they'll manage to get it pushed through one of these days. And we all know what'll happen then. The crazies will still manage to get all the guns they want and law-abiding citizens who only want a little protection won't be able to get one for nothin'.''

Lynn switched pots on the coffee machine and wiped up a few stains with her cloth. It was all just so much background noise. She didn't really even listen to the blaring television or the philosophizing customers attentively; the conversations didn't vary much.

The newcaster continued. "The President escaped serious injury when he was knocked to the floor by the quick action of Senator Daniel Resnick of Illinois, who was also in attendance. Before he could be stopped, the gunman, identified only as a white male in his late twenties, fired twice, seriously injuring Senator Resnick, who was rushed immediately to Walter Reed Hospital. Details on the extent of his injury will be brought to you when we have more information.''

She stared at the flickering television screen and wasn't sure her heart didn't stop entirely for a second or two. Dan. That was all she could think of. Dan was hurt.

"Hey, Lynn, how about another cup of coffee? Tastes good on a cold night.''

Gerald, the balding owner of Chubb's, who didn't normally work nights, was there because the night cook hadn't been able to make it in to work. He watched Lynn standing with an empty coffee decanter in one hand and a wet cloth in the other. In a moment's time, her face had lost all its color and was as white as her blouse and apron.

"Lynn, are you all right? The man wants some coffee."

She heard him, yet she couldn't move. She just stood there watching the television, which had returned to some action-adventure show.

"Lynn?" her boss asked more forcefully. "Are you okay?"

She turned to him, and her dark eyes were as large as saucers, threatening to take over her chalky face. "No," she replied in a strangled voice. "No, I'm not all right."

"Hey," he said, placing a hand on her elbow and steering her toward one of the stools at the counter. "Sit down, take it easy a minute. I'll take the guy his coffee."

He returned in a few seconds and sat down beside her on the next stool. "Flu bug hit you all of a sudden?"

Lynn closed her eyes as if she were in pain. And, in a way, she was. In fact, she would have welcomed physical pain in the place of what she was feeling now.

She shook her head and looked at the homely man. In his gruff way, he had been very kind to her. He deserved a bit of honesty. It would be easy to admit to the flu bug and run off home to huddle in front of the ancient black and white set in her apartment to chew her fingernails down to the quick while she waited for news of Dan's condition.

"I know him," she said weakly.

"Huh?"

"Senator Resnick, the man who was shot in Washington. I know him well. It's quick a shock."

Gerald looked at her with a mixture of surprise, pity, and curiosity. "On close terms with a senator, huh? I always knew you didn't belong in a place like this. Rough world, isn't it, kid? I think I get the picture. He's married and can't or won't

114

get a divorce because of his career, so you came running off to this neck of the woods to get him out of your system.''

If Lynn hadn't been so upset, she would have laughed. Gerald, despite his rough exterior, was no fool. His assumption was a sharp one . . . and a natural one. "You're close to the truth," she admitted, her voice and color returning slowly, "but he isn't married and neither am I. But I *am* here to get him out of my system. And to let me get out of his.''

He patted her arm in an awkward but sympathetic way. "Well, let's hope he'll be okay. But I got a feelin', Lynn, that dying's the only way a man could get you out of his system, once you got a hold on him. You're quite a girl. Love him?''

Somehow the question didn't seem probing or out of place. Lynn looked at Gerald and nodded as scalding hot tears rolled down her face.

"Then I suppose . . .''

Before he could complete his comment, another news bulletin flashed on the screen. Microphones had been placed in front of a sober-countenanced doctor on the steps of the hospital.

"What can you tell us about Senator Resnick's condition, Dr. Gentry?''

"He took two bullets, both in the chest. One lodged in the pleura of the right lung. The other shattered some bone in the left rib cage which was, in its way, fortunate, because this was the only factor that kept the bullet from entering the heart itself. He was in surgery quite some time to remove the bullets. Damage to surrounding tissues was repaired and the bone fragments were also removed. There was quite significant blood loss and he's had several blood transfusions. Senator Resnick's condition is critical but stable. At this time, it's impossible to speculate. He will, of course, be kept in intensive care until all danger is past.''

"Is this, then, a life-threatening situation?'' the news reporter asked.

The physician appeared irritated by the question, showing

that he felt he had answered it already as well as he could.

"We'll keep the media posted on the senator's condition as we know more about it. He isn't out of danger, but he is young and strong and in excellent general condition. All of that is in his favor. That's all I can tell you at this time. Now, if you'll excuse me please . . ."

The tears continued to roll down Lynn's face as she listened silently. He was alive, but he wasn't out of danger. What if he died thinking she didn't love him, that she was a shallow person incapable of returning his love? She thought of that hateful letter she had written and her heart was rent in two.

"Hey," Gerald said, placing his hands on her shoulders. The customers were staring at them but Lynn didn't care, "look, if you need to leave, if you want to go see the guy, then take off. We'll find a way to make it. Don't worry about it, okay?"

Lynn's mind was working feverishly. If she could only go . . . even just long enough to know for sure that he was going to be okay. She could do that, then quietly drift away again. But she had to find a way to let him know she cared about him. A telephone call wouldn't get through. Probably a telegram wouldn't either. And a letter would take too long. Besides, he would be flooded with letters from well-wishers from all over the country. Hers might never reach him.

As she tended to do when she was deeply worried, she folded her hands in her lap and stared down at them. "I just don't know what to do, Gerald. The only way I could get there in a short time is to fly. With the roads the way they are, I'd never get to the airport in my little car."

"Hey, Ken," called out Gerald to one of the customers, "aren't you pulling out toward Little Rock?"

"Sure thing. Soon I'll have that eighteen-wheeler singin' down the highway just as sweet as if that white stuff wasn't there."

"You get in any trouble if you give a lady a lift? This little gal needs to get to the airport."

Big, burly Ken didn't even think it over twice. "Hell, I'm

not supposed to give people rides. None of us are. But we do all the time anyway. And if I was ever gonna break a rule, I'd do it for a girl as pretty as Lynn. You got any getting ready to do, kid?"

"When do you need to leave?" she asked quickly.

He glanced down at his watch and said, "Fifteen minutes. Don't have to be rigid. Can't hold a guy to a strict timetable during these conditions."

"I just have to go to my place, throw a few things in a bag. If you'll drop me by there to do that, I promise I won't take long. And I'll pay you well for this."

The truck driver appeared embarrassed. "Don't you go worryin' about pay and all that. If I can help you out, then that's all I want out of it."

Lynn turned back toward the restaurant owner. "I hate to leave you in the lurch like this . . ."

He shrugged diffidently. "Don't sweat it. Business is lousy anyway. By the time the weather clears, I'll hire someone else. Waitresses, cooks, dishwashers. They all come and go. You get used to it. Some you hate to see go more than others, though. And it's no secret that I think you're special. I'll miss you, girl."

She looked at him in surprise, "But I'll be back in a few days, Gerald. Just as soon as I see what's really going on with him. I guess you know as well as I do that I won't be staying here in Radley forever, but I'll come back and work till you find someone else."

"Better stay with your man," he said gently.

She shook her head and swallowed the bitterness that had risen up in her throat. "It isn't possible. That's why I'm here in the first place. But thanks ever so much for letting me go tonight. It's awfully sweet of you, and I'll never forget it." Leaning over slightly, she gave him a brief hug and watched him blush a beet red. Looking back over at the truck driver, she said, "I'll get my things and will be ready whenever you are."

Ken assisted her up into the huge truck and followed her

directions to where she lived. While she hurried about in the apartment, she could hear the hum of the big engine against the cold night air. She didn't even take time to change clothes. Moving as quickly as she could, she gathered up some toilet articles, a flannel nightgown, and a change of clothing. At the last moment, on a sudden impulse, she picked up Herbie and placed him in the overnight case where he glistened and gleamed because the engagement ring Dan had given her was on a chain around his neck. She had often toyed with the idea of returning it, of sending it back to Dan by registered, insured mail, but she kept putting it off and it was still with her. In a corner of her mind, she had nurtured the idea that Dan might see her as mercenary if she kept the obviously expensive diamond . . . and that idea might cool his ardor toward her as much as anything else.

"Boy, you are quick," the man called Ken said in surprise when Lynn opened the door of the truck and scrambled up. "From what I know of women, I was prepared to park here for ages while you decided what to take."

Lynn managed a little laugh. "I'll probably wish, when morning comes, that I had taken more time. But it isn't important. If I need something I didn't bring, I can buy it there."

The truck driver turned the radio up high to a station that played country music. Lynn sat perched on the edge of the seat, looking way down at the highway, and listening to songs of cheating, beer drinking, and good love gone bad. Only twice during the entire ride was there any news of Dan. Recalling past presidential assassination attempts, Lynn mused that mere senators didn't rate that much furor. Or perhaps that wasn't being fair. Maybe this particular station just didn't lean toward frequent news bulletins. It was late, very late, and it was a small-town station.

"We're just a few miles out of Little Rock," Ken remarked. "You have any idea when you can get a plane to where you're going?"

Lynn shook her head even though he couldn't see her in the

dark cab, then said, "I didn't take time to call and check. It didn't matter, really. This was the best way I had of getting there so I didn't turn it down. If there isn't a flight out for a while, I'll be safe and warm there. But I hope it isn't long. Not because I mind to sit there, but because this is terribly important. I can't be too late. I just can't be."

She wasn't sure why, being a normally reticent person, she had almost poured her heart out to Gerald and Ken, two men she barely knew. Ken hadn't asked any questions. She didn't know if he had overheard any of her conversation with Gerald or not. It didn't matter. Nothing mattered but Dan's life and well-being.

He seemed reluctant to leave her alone at the airport. When she insisted he gave in, but he did adamantly refuse to take any money from her.

Her mind kept up a silent prayer, a litany that went on and on, as she made her way to the ticket desk. The clerk, moved from passivity by her urgency, looked at her and said in a kind voice, "I'll do some checking for you, ma'am. A lot of flights have been canceled, but we can surely find one for you. Probably, this kind of weather, they won't all be booked solid."

In a few moments, he turned his attention back away from the computerized flight schedules that were ever-changing and said, "Can you be ready in an hour?"

"I'm ready now," she said simply. He named the amount of the fare and she counted the payment out to him in cash. He looked at the green and white bills in surprise, then glanced back up at her. "Look, if you're carrying much more of that, you better hide it well. Especially when you get into D.C. Airports late at night . . . young ladies traveling alone. Be careful."

Lynn felt a sob rising in her throat at his kind concern. When she had no one to really see after her, the casual comments of strangers were most welcome. "Thanks," she managed to say. "I'll be careful. And I don't have much more cash."

While she sat down to wait, she pondered the truth of that

statement. She *didn't* have much more cash. And she certainly didn't want to go writing personal checks in Washington, D.C. or registering at a hotel where she had to give her name and address, but she'd have to stay somewhere while she was there. Then, too, she'd have to buy a ticket back to Arkansas. Personal checks could trace her. Well, she would just have to figure that out later. Lynn Marsh had never applied for a credit card because they asked too many questions on the application blanks. It was awkward, but she would manage somehow. She always had.

At long last, she was aboard the plane. Fear churned inside her. Fear for Dan. There was one stopover in Memphis, Tennessee, which was of longer duration than the flight itself. Lynn bought a magazine from a stand at the airport, but the black letters danced in front of her eyes without coherence. Strangers passed by. She paid no attention to them and they paid no attention to her. Once a young man, possibly not even out of his teens, paused and gave her a keen appraisal. Instead of feeling afraid of him, Lynn looked down at the portable radio and cassette player he was carrying. "Have you had that on recently?" she asked.

He stopped his leering, obviously taken aback because she was talking to him without hesitation. A beautiful woman in an expensive coat . . . that sort wasn't usually too anxious to associate with him. "Off and on," he answered laconically.

"Have you heard anything lately about Senator Resnick?"

The young man pushed back a lock of slightly greasy hair and looked at her blankly.

"Senator Resnick," she repeated impatiently. "The man who was shot in Washington, D.C."

"Oh, yeah, the guy who played hero. Some sap. I'd-a let 'em shoot the guy. Maybe done us all a favor." He paused, took in Lynn's stricken face and gave in. "Last I heard, he was still alive. There probably won't be much news till morning. I mean, I guess it is morning, but you know what I mean."

Lynn nodded and sat back down in the plastic seat. Two A.M

might technically be considered morning, but it was the dead of night to her. She felt gray and lifeless, and a hateful dampness seemed to cling to her clothing and hair. When she went to the ladies' room to freshen up, she could still smell the odors of frying bacon and hamburgers as she combed her hair. The pale, big-eyed face that stared back at her from the mirror was a stranger's face. It was the face of a woman who had told the most wonderful man in the world that she wasn't really serious about him, that she had only been playing a game. How could she have done that? How, oh God, how? Then it had seemed so right. It had been the only thing she could think of to do for Dan's own good. Now it seemed so heartless. If he had cared at all—and she knew he had—then he was lying there critically wounded and maybe she was on his mind. And it couldn't be good what he was thinking. If he had been emotionally wounded enough, he might even be wanting to die. Or not fighting as much as he should. She had heard that mental attitude was so important.

Soon she was back on the plane. When it landed again, she was in Washington. Her plans had not extended beyond that. What was she to do now? How on earth was she going to persuade someone to let her see Dan, let her get a message to him?

She squared her chin and moved it defiantly upward. She had made it here, hadn't she? That was the biggest task. Picking up her one bag, she looked in her purse, counted the few remaining bills, and ran out to hail a taxi. At least Washington wasn't like Radley, Arkansas, and taxis were always available around the airport.

"Walter Reed Hospital," she told the driver, then settled down in the back seat. The lights of the nation's capital flashed by the car windows in a blur. She saw nothing. She heard nothing. All her heart, soul, mind, and body were concentrating on one thing and one thing only: Dan.

Chapter Eight

WHEN THE TAXI pulled up at the hospital, Lynn got out and paid the driver, adding a tip which brought a broad smile to his face she was too preoccupied to notice. She entered the huge facility and hunted up the information desk. It was five-ten A.M. and the business office wasn't exactly bustling. A tired-looking woman turned away from a confessions magazine she was reading long enough to ask Lynn if she could help her.

"Senator Resnick's room number."

The clerk's mouth drew into a tight, forbidding line. "I'm not allowed to give out that information."

"But, please—it's so vitally important. I don't even need to see him, just leave a message."

The woman shook her head with grim determination. "Even if I were to give you the information, it wouldn't help. The entire floor is under heavy security. In addition, the senator is still in intensive care, and no visitors are allowed except close family members."

Nodding to show she understood, Lynn moved away. She didn't know what step to take next, but the clerk had given Lynn more help than she realized, for she had divulged the information that Dan was still alive. If Lynn could just now find a way to get a message to him, then if she had to give him up to death, she would at least know he hadn't died believing she didn't care for him deeply.

Five-fifteen A.M. What an hour to be roaming around at loose ends in a strange city. Lynn considered finding a nearby hotel and booking a room for the day and night. She could at least freshen up, take a bath, change clothes, and maybe even have a nap before she caught a flight back home. The problems connected with finding a way to pay for the room were too weighty, however. Feeling small, lost, and very much alone, she hunted up the public rest room at the hospital. To her relief, it was empty. The hospital wasn't abounding with visitors at such an ungodly hour.

Taking her small overnight case with her, she stepped into one of the stalls and changed her clothes. She felt better once she was wearing brown wool slacks, a peach-colored blouse, and dressy suede shoes. Under the harsh artificial lights of the restroom, she winced at her own pale, woebegone appearance. After brushing her hair, she withdrew a cosmetics bag from her purse and attacked her face with determination. On most occasions, Lynn wore little makeup; but today, she thought grimly, she needed all the help she could get.

Glancing at her watch, she sighed. Although time was precious, she wanted to go about this the right way. She decided that waiting until at least seven A.M. would be to her benefit when it came to approaching the police guards. She strolled through the hospital corridors and located the cafeteria and snack bar. Both were still closed. Locating the vending machines, she despondently fed change into them, ending up with a cup of black coffee so strong it could have stood without the styrofoam cup and something in a cellophane wrapper that vaguely resembled a Danish pastry. She wasn't hungry and had purchased the items more to pass the time than for any other reason. However, when she settled down on the vinyl chair in the waiting room and began to sip the coffee and nibble at the stale roll, she was surprised at the welcome her empty stomach gave the bit of warmth and nourishment. She supposed that her overwrought emotional state had made her forget her physical needs. The fact remained that her body needed food and rest.

The minutes ticked by like hours. When seven o'clock finally arrived, Lynn lost her courage and decided to wait awhile longer. There still wasn't much activity from where she sat, and she talked herself into believing she would stand a better chance to getting a message through to Dan if she waited for a more "normal" hour. At eight o'clock, she knew she was being foolish. There was no point in putting it off longer. In fact, she really should have gone ahead earlier. There might have been an edge to presenting herself at five o'clock that would have spoken of urgency and earnestness. It was too late to think of that now. Gathering up all the courage she possessed, along with her purse and overnight bag, she went in search of the "secret" floor and corridor that held Dan Resnick.

As she walked down the halls, head held high, she noticed that a gift shop was being unlocked and opened for the day. On impulse, she walked inside and purchased a single red rose, a terribly corny get-well card, and one of those wooden paddles with a small rubber ball attached to it by a long elastic string. The information desk had undergone a personnel change but not a policy change. The new clerk had orders not to divulge information about Dan's location either.

Heavy coat slung over one arm, bags hanging from the other, Lynn got on the nearest elevator and started working her way up, stopping at every floor, then walking down every corridor. It shouldn't be *that* difficult to locate the general vicinity, since it would be heavily guarded and, possibly, heavily populated with representatives of the news media. Reporters had a way of ferreting out information that ordinary individuals couldn't.

Her feet and legs were already aching when she got off on the eighth floor. As soon as she stepped out of the elevator onto the polished tile floor, she knew. She knew Dan was close by even before she walked down the hall, heels tapping against the hard surface, and saw the throng of people, mostly male and mostly in uniform.

As she had anticipated, when she drew too close she was stopped immediately and eyed with hostile suspicion.

"You can't come through here, miss," a blue-uniformed man said sternly.

Seeming to comply, Lynn stepped back. Arranging the various things she had to carry was somewhat awkward. Out of view of the sharp-eyed strangers, she placed her traveling bag on the floor and folded her coat on top of it. Opening her purse, she searched for a pen and scrawled across the bottom of the silly card:

Dan,
Impossible though it may be for you to believe me after what I did to hurt you, I love you. We still can't be together, but you're tough and strong. You have to beat this thing: for yourself and for the people you serve so faithfully—and for me. As as long as I know you're in the world, I don't feel so alone. If you give up and die, a part of me will die along with you, perhaps the most important part, for I truly love you more than myself—more than life itself. Memories of you keep me going at times when it would be infinitely simpler to give up.

Lynn

It was incongruous, she thought, to place such a dramatic message at the bottom of a comical card picturing odd-looking toads and turtles. Hoping no one was watching her because her actions seemed absurd to her, she placed her coat back over her arm and searched through the weekender bag until she found Herbie Bear wearing his diamond necklace. She placed the bear and the card into the brown bag bearing the Bo-Lo bat and the rose with its long stem encased in green florist's paper.

Taking small, tentative steps, she moved slowly back to the forbidden area. From a safe distance, she watched the crowd, hoping to find a kind face. Or at least a weak face—anyone at all with whom she might stand a chance. Her dark eyes lit on a stocky man who ws probably approaching the age of retirement. Although he was wearing a plain gray suit and conservative shirt and tie, he seemed to be in command of things. An FBI agent. A plainclothes policeman. His face looked intelligent, tired, and compassionate. Despite his obvious authority, he wasn't unapproachable. Heart in her throat, Lynn walked closer to the crowded area. The same uniformed man spotted her, sighed wearily, and walked to where she stood.

"You might as well go home, miss. You won't be allowed any closer."

"I'm a very close friend of Dan's . . . Senator Resnick's. If you were to ask him, I'm sure—"

"No one is allowed in but immediate family," he retorted sharply. "Are you immediate family? Don't go telling me you're his little sister."

At any other time, the man's rudeness would have angered Lynn. Now she just accepted it as a part of what she had to endure. When she did not reply immediately, his eyes looked her up and down insolently. He didn't need to speak his thoughts. They were very apparent to Lynn. He saw her as an adoring fan of the handsome politician . . . *or* a casual light-o'-love in his life.

She stood her ground firmly, gave the rude man the full effect of her most haughtily aristocratic stare. It wasn't a tactic she used often, but it never failed to make an impact. The guard seemed to take a new look at this attractive young woman who wasn't being intimidated by his high-handed sarcasm. "Actually," she said, using her best finishing-school-type voice, "there isn't any need for me to see Senator Resnick personally. I realize he is still in intensive care, and the last thing I want would be to do something detrimental to his well-being." With a nod toward the gray-suited man, she told the guard, "Would you please have that man come over here?"

He stared at her, openly incredulous. "That's Lemuel Hasty."

"And?"

"He's a wheel in the FBI, pretty much running this show. What makes you think he'd talk to you?"

"I don't know that he will," she replied simply. "I only requested that you ask that he come over here. Whether you wish to believe it or not, I do know the senator very well. If I choose to tell him, he won't be pleased with the way in which I've been treated.''

Murmuring something under his breath which she felt it was just as well she didn't catch, the uniformed man walked away from her and exchanged words with the older man in the conservative suit. He looked over to Lynn, shrugged his heavy shoulders, and started walking toward her.

''What did you need, young lady?''

''I'm not asking to see Senator Resnick. I only ask that this be delivered to him as soon as possible.'' She hesitantly held up the brown sack with the rose sticking way out of the top.

Lemuel Hasty was a man accustomed to assessing human character quickly and accurately. If he hadn't possessed that facility, he wouldn't be where he was now. He saw a very pretty woman who, despite obvious tiredness, had taken care with her appearance. Under less hectic circumstances, she would have had all male heads turning her direction. Beyond that, he saw her goodness and strength. He also saw a depth of pain in her eyes that was raw and aching. ''I don't suppose,'' he said, his voice almost kind, ''that you'd consider telling me your name.''

''He'll know. And my name would mean nothing to you.'' Silently, she added, but my previous name, Linda Marshall, would make you sit up and take notice.

His steely yet kind gaze raked across her finely molded features and again probed the deep brown eyes. She had a pretty face, sure enough, but he wasn't a sucker for pretty faces. He couldn't afford to be. Still, there was something about her . . . something he trusted with an intuition that was keener than intellect.

''I'll see that he gets the package, ma'am. But it *will* have to go through security clearance first. You can understand the reasons for that, can't you?''

''I understand. And I don't mind. But please do it as quickly as possible. I couldn't bear it if he died before seeing it. And, naturally, no one will tell me how close to death he is.''

"He's holding his own, but it could still go either way. He's unconscious at the moment but his vital signs are good. Anything he needs, he's getting it. It would have been that way anyway, but the President is making sure. After all, he owes this man his life."

Lynn's surprise at Mr. Hasty's revelation about Dan's condition must have showed in her eyes. He smiled a slight smile that barely made his thin lips curve. "Now you can't say no one told you anything. I certainly said more than I'm supposed to say."

"Why?" she asked, regarding him gravely.

He lifted his shaggy eyebrows and shrugged. "I have this strange feeling that there is more to you than meets the eye. Not that what meets the eye is bad. Your parcel, young lady?"

She hesitated for a moment, then reached down into the sack to take out the card. "He won't need this," she explained. "He'll know and understand. Thank you, Mr. Hasty. Thank you so very much." With that, she handed the sack to the older man.

Just as she was preparing to turn and walk away, she glanced down the hall and saw a man open a door and come out into the corridor. He was shorter than Dan, with a more stocky frame, and a good deal older. He was a stranger to Lynn, for she had never seen him before, yet he was familiar. He had very black hair mixed with a generous amount of silver. His eyes were an unusual gray . . . at the moment quite deep and grave, yet she knew those eyes could twinkle with laughter, turn slate hard with anger. Perhaps he sensed her staring at him because he turned to look at her as if pulled by a magnet too strong to be defied. Odd though it was, she found herself smiling at him. The corners of his eyes crinkled with curiosity but he returned her smile with a slightly crooked one of his own—and that crooked smile was also familiar. She had seen one like it quite often on Dan's face.

He took a step toward her as if he were considering approaching her. Taking one last look at him, Lynn turned, picked up her few possessions, and walked swiftly away. She didn't feel safe until she was in the elevator moving downward toward the first floor.

Back up on the heavily guarded corridor of the eighth floor, the dark-haired, gray-eyed man went up to Lemuel Hasty and said, "Who was that young woman?"

"She didn't seem to want to say, Mr. Resnick. She just wanted me to make sure your son gets this as quickly as possible. Of course, it'll have to go to the lab and have a security check run first."

"May I see?" Bill Resnick asked.

Hasty handed him the paper sack which was becoming worn and soft around the top. Bill Resnick paid no attention to the rose, gave the Bo-Lo bat a curious glance, then withdrew the little brown bear from the parcel. "Herbie," he said in awe, fingering the ring hanging from a chain around the toy's neck. Even a quick glance at the diamond let him know roughly what it was worth. That was a lot of carats for a balding teddy bear well over thirty years old to wear.

"Herbie?" queried Hasty.

"He was Dan's when he was just a little boy. A great favorite. In fact, he kept sleeping with Herbie long after he was ashamed to admit he did so. I didn't even know the crazy bear still existed."

Hasty wasn't sure what was going on. He was even less sure he wanted to get involved. "Well," he announced in businesslike tones, "I'll have one of the boys run the stuff over to headquarters to be checked out. Anything could be sewn inside that stuffed toy."

Resnick clutched Lynn's package possessively against his chest. "I don't think that will be necessary, Hasty. If Herbie has survived this long, I think he deserves more than having his stuffing all pulled out."

"But it's orders," Hasty protested.

"I'll take the responsibility, Mr. Hasty. You're a good man.

Check the rest of them out according to all rules and regulations. Something tells me I better get this package where it belongs as quickly as possible. It just might be what my son needs. Dan hasn't been himself for a long, long time. And I worry that he's not fighting this thing as hard as he should.''

Before the FBI agent could object further, the father of the heroic senator from Illinois walked back into the cloistered hospital room. His wife, a woman with a careworn face, sat on a stiff-backed chair watching the silent form on the snowy white linens.

''He hasn't moved much, Bill,'' she said tonelessly. ''I think —I can almost feel it—that he hears me when I talk, but he just doesn't bother to reply. It's almost as if he's given up. But our Dan isn't like that. He was never a quitter.''

The older man slowly approached the metal hospital bed. Reaching down, he smoothed back the lock of black hair that had fallen across Dan's forehead. He handed the single rose to his wife. ''Maybe when a nurse's aide comes in, she can find you a bud vase for that.'' Without further explanation, he continued to withdraw the contents of the sack. He placed the silly wooden paddle and rubber ball on the bedside table.

''What is all this stuff?'' Irene Resnick asked. ''Who on earth would send him a child's toy at such a time?''

Still not talking, Bill Resnick took the shabby Herbie Bear out, then crumpled the sack and threw it in the nearby waste receptacle.

''Herbie!'' she exclaimed, weary eyes brightening momentarily with surprise. ''I don't understand all this.''

''Neither do I,'' her husband said softly. ''But I'm hoping there's a key here to explain his recent unhappiness, his inability to fight back at his injuries as he should. A very lovely young woman brought them here, Irene. Look at that diamond around Herbie Bear's neck.''

Irene did and uttered a soft gasp.

Bill Resnick took the bear, diamond and all, and placed him

within his son's arm. He smoothed back the hair again. The memories came flooding back. Once this man hadn't been a powerful senator. Once he had been a small boy called Danny who was as tough as any boy, yet had an awfully hard time giving up his teddy bear.

In the meantime, Lynn had reached the main floor and ran gratefully out into the cold, wintry air. She had accomplished her purpose. Pausing for a moment, she took the silly get-well card, tore it into many tiny pieces, and tossed the pieces into a litter barrel on the corner. She was glad she hadn't left the card behind. Putting what she felt into words simply wasn't possible. Nothing sounded adequate or suitable. A red rose was the symbol of true love. The Bo-Lo bat would show she remembered and treasured his silly gifts. Herbie Bear would prove that she had cared enough not to discard him and had returned him to the rightful owner in his time of need. The diamond ring on a chain would let Dan know she hadn't sold it for easy cash. That was enough to tell him she cared without mere words that came out stilted and overly dramatic.

The corner where she had discarded the fragments of the card also held a bench with a strange-looking metal wall behind it, perhaps designed to bear the brunt of some of the winter winds. Lynn looked at the faded schedule, corners curling, and saw that the bus would be by in ten minutes and would take her to the airport. Since it would be much less expensive than a taxi, she sat down on the cold, hard bench to wait. How she wished that she had had more warning for this, had a chance to withdraw more cash from the bank. The problem still remained of finding a way to pay for the air fare back to Little Rock, then of finding transportation from Little Rock to Radley.

She had never thought she would be glad to see that shabby apartment and the homely greasy-spoon cafe and truckstop. But she would be. She was bone-tired and still had no assurance that Dan, her love, would be all right. The bus pulled up at the corner. Just as Lynn was entering its door with several other passengers, she took one look at the hospital. The man she had assumed was Dan's father was running down the steps. He looked almost frantically from side to side, then let his shoulders sag in weary resignation, and walked back into the hospital.

Lynn wanted to huddle in the back of the bus and cry. She wouldn't, however, let herself indulge in the luxury of tears. Not yet. She had to get away from here before she was found by Dan's family. Or even worse—she shuddered at the thought—by the FBI. This trip had been foolish, really. The latest photographs they possessed of her showed her still in her teens, yet there was always a chance someone sharp enough would recognize her as Davy Marshall's daughter and all that harassment would begin again.

At the airport, she wrote a check for her fare. In no time at all, she had a ticket back to Arkansas in her hand and was making her way to the designated gate. At the end of the flight, which seemed inordinately long and turbulent, she found she had enough cash left for a bus ticket from Little Rock to a town a few miles outside of Radley. Getting from there to Radley shouldn't be hard. If necessary, she could call Gerald and he could come get her or send one of the waitresses who wasn't working that shift. That left two dollars and thirty-four cents in her purse. Her stomach growled audibly, and she was aware of its neglect and emptiness. With the little bit of remaining money, she purchased a sandwich and a small carton of milk from a machine and consumed them while she waited the seemingly endless hours for the bus that would take her from Little Rock to Briarcliff. When she was on board at last, she leaned back against the seat. If she had expected to sleep, she was fooled. Rest was elusive. Her mind was too feverish with worry over Dan. She was glad she had seen his father. Of course, she couldn't be sure of that. The man could have been an uncle or a much older brother. At least Dan had family with him, and that was important.

The big bus jerked to a stop at Briarcliff, still a small town but twice the size of Radley—and nearly thirty miles away. With sinking heart, she dialed the number of Chubb's. Carol Ann, one of the other waitresses, answered.

"Carol Ann? I'm at the bus station in Briarcliff and I don't have a way home. Could you get hold of Gerald for me and see if he could spare someone to come after me? I'll pay them well just as soon as I can get to the bank."

"Look, Lynn, you okay?"

"I'm okay. I'm just tired and ready to come home."

"Well, Gerald's here. I'll let you talk to him."

When she explained the situation, he said quickly, "I'll be right there."

"If you're busy, send someone else, Gerald. I know you have a lot to do."

"Forget it. Say, by the way, just heard a news bulletin. They say your senator is improving. Not exactly ready to hold a full-scale press conference, but awake and talking, moving around."

Lynn sent up a grateful little prayer and had a hard time getting out the "Thanks for telling me" in a coherent enough way that it could be understood.

"You look terrible" was Gerald's first comment to her when he saw her some time later.

"Thanks for cheering me up," she said wryly. "Does that mean you're not going to make me go into work tonight?"

"Way you look, you'd scare them off. They'd take one look at you and think you had some contagious disease. Take a couple of days off, catch up on your rest, then give me a call and I'll tell you what the schedule's like."

How she managed it, she wasn't sure, but Lynn did stumble up the steep stairs to her place, slip out of her clothing and into the wrinkled flannel gown she had carried with her to Washington and not worn. When she hit the bed, she was instantly asleep and stayed that way all evening, all night, and well into the next day.

The first thing she did when she woke up was to switch on the small television set. She had to wait through a myriad of soap operas and game shows, but finally found a news program that informed her Senator Daniel Resnick of Illinois was improving rapidly and had been moved from the intensive care unit. She sobbed with relief.

At that same moment, this said young senator was sitting up in bed surrounded by his parents, two physicians, Lemuel Hasty, and his best friend, adviser, and campaign manager, Patrick O'Donnell.

"There's a young woman named Lynn Marsh who, until the past few months, lived in a small town in the Missouri Ozarks called St. Clair. She owned a cabin and a piece of property next to Jess Wicklein's. She also managed—owned—a novelty, gift, and antique shop called The Calico Cat. I want her found."

"Quit moving around so abruptly," one doctor said.

Dan glared at him. He was definitely getting better.

"I want her found. I have no idea where she is. She may even be using a different name. But I do want her found. And hang the cost."

Patrick O'Donnell admonished, "You're getting too excited, Dan. You need to take it easy. There's not a lot to be gained by sending a bunch of people off on what will probably prove to be a wild-goose chase. If this young woman doesn't want to be found, then she probably won't be."

"Hogwash," he announced inelegantly, looking over at the veteran FBI man. "Hasty, do me a favor. Locate her. I want to know everything about her there is to know."

"Dan—" Hasty began to protest feebly.

"Do it, or I'll get out of this bed right this minute and begin the search myself. And charge the expenses up to me. We can't have the taxpayers footing a bill because I can't seem to handle my love life."

"Dan," his father began carefully, "maybe it would be best to let it go. Sure, she cared enough to come see about you. The fact remains that she did leave. There must be a reason for that.''

The dignified senator from Illinois reached out and touched the teddy bear which remained by his side in the hospital bed. "Then I intend to know that reason. Enough is enough. She loves me. She always did. It was just pride that kept me from completely disregarding that idiotic letter she wrote me. But I feel it. I know it. And another woman can never matter to me in the way she does. Find her. To hell with the costs. To hell with the consequences.''

Patrick O'Donnell and Lemuel Hasty exchanged glances, nodded almost imperceptibly at each other, and then looked back at the determined Daniel Resnick.

"She'll be found,'' Hasty said shortly.

Lynn had only been back at work at Chubb's three days when they descended upon her. The large, dark-colored, four-door cars pulled up outside the little truckstop, and the men in conservative suits and white shirts began to pour out and walk toward the restaurant door. She recognized their sort immediately. The undercover ones could fool you. But these all had the same look about them. She suppressed the urge to run wildly toward the back door. From past experience, she was willing to bet more agents were stationed there.

"Miss Marshall,'' one tall man said in a voice that wasn't really harsh at all, "you'll have to come with us. You don't have to be afraid, but we do have some questions to ask.''

Lynn nodded in resignation while the restaurant personnel and customers gaped at the scene in amazement. This was the most exciting event that had hit Radley since the mayor split his britches during his Founders' Day speech. It might even top the time the conservative Presbyterian minister had run off with Debbie Jennings, a girl just barely out of high school who had a reputation for being fast.

"Well, Gerald,'' she quipped, trying for levity even though

her dark eyes were wide with apprehension, "it looks as if I'm leaving you in the lurch again. This time it's probably for good."

"They're not arresting you, are they, Lynn?" he asked, obviously horrified at the thought.

Lynn looked at the bevy of federal agents. "Are you?" she queried, lifting her delicately arched brows at them.

The tall one, who seemed to be the spokesman, replied in carefully measured words, "You aren't being arrested. We merely request that you come with us for questioning. If it's any comfort to you, you'll be allowed to pack what you need to bring with you. It might also interest you to know that we'll be stopping at a hospital in the District of Columbia before any intensive questioning is performed."

"He's okay?" she asked, her voice barely above a whisper.

"Mending fast and doing quite well. Well enough to be imperious. You hid your tracks quite well, Miss Marshall. Finding Lynn Marsh wasn't hard. Going beyond that was extremely difficult."

"Then why did you bother?" she inquired wearily. "It scarcely seems worth the effort. I can tell you nothing you don't already know about my father and his operations."

"A certain senator was most insistent," the man answered her, actually giving a ghost of a smile.

"He'll be sorry."

The big man shrugged. "That's out of my territory. I did as I was instructed. What happens now is out of my hands."

Before she left, Lynn said good-bye to everyone in the cafe. She hugged homely Gerald for a moment and whispered, "I promise I'll write or call and explain this whole situation. But I'm no criminal. You can believe that."

"I believe it," he said firmly, something that suspiciously resembled a tear floating across his eye as he broke away from her embrace.

The trunks of the three large federal cars held all of Lynn's possessions from the upstairs rooms. "What about my car?" she asked. "I don't suppose you trust me to drive it. For all you know, I'd break away from you in heavy traffic and head toward Sheboygan."

One of the younger agents hid a grin by placing a hand in front of his face. "I'll drive your car, Miss Marshall, and you can ride with my partner."

"We're driving all the way to Washington, D.C.?" she asked, still not believing this was happening.

That's what they did, however.

The drive went on forever. Stops were made only when totally necessary for fuel. Eating and calls of nature had to be synchronized with these pit stops. What little sleep they got was obtained sitting up on the passenger sides of the big cars.

Not entirely heartless, they checked Lynn into a nice hotel and let her take a long, soaking bath and change into clean clothes. While she was doing that, two agents stood guard outside the main door She felt penned in and trapped. It wasn't a good feeling.

They had promised her she would see Dan, and she wanted to look her best. She felt a glow of impish pleasure at sending one of the burly agents off with a brightly colored dress across his arm in search of someone in the hotel who would press the wrinkles out of it for her. When he returned, sheepishly holding out the dress, she was done with her hair and makeup. Going into the bathroom, she took off her terry-cloth bathrobe and slipped into the emerald green dress with lavish touches of white lace.

Reporters were swarming all around the hotel and were even thicker outside the hospital. Lynn shuddered involuntarily as the microphones were thrust her way and all their questions came at one time. It reminded her of that terrible day nearly nine years ago when a similar bunch had descended on the lawn of her private school in St. Louis. Only the names and faces were different.

The agents managed to squeeze past the eager press and into

the hospital. She was escorted swiftly back up to the eighth floor. Her heart was beating rapidly against her soft breasts. What was she going to say to him? She expected to see him still reclining in bed, pale and pajama-clad. Instead, he sat perched on the edge of the bed, fully dressed in a tweed blazer and wool slacks. He was somewhat pale and thin, but he was her Dan. Lynn stared at him, drinking in every feature, every line of his tall body, and didn't say a word.

"Welcome back, my Lynn. I've missed you more than words can express."

Tears came unbidden to her eyes. "Oh, Dan, what have you done? Do you know the whole story about me? Now you can surely see why—"

"I see why you thought so," he said gently. He looked about at the federal men, at his family members, at the white-clad, hovering nurse. "I'd like to talk to Lynn alone. You may all wait right outside the door if you wish. This won't take long."

He stood up, looking taller than she had recalled, perhaps because he was now so thin.

"I won't go on living my life without you, Lynn. That's something you might as well accept."

She longed to seek the comfort of his arms but held back. "Don't you see how impossible it is? It will ruin your career. People, so many of them, will be ready to believe you were part of the syndicate my father headed. Even if they retain their faith in you, I'll drag you down, for they'll never believe I didn't know, wasn't a party to it."

"Did you know, Lynn? Were you his confidante? Did he tell you where the missing cash and jewels are?"

She shook her head. "He was just my daddy. Anything I wanted, I had. Mother too. He was a king, and he treated us like his queen and princess. But we had no idea what kind of kingdom he ruled. Now the hounding will start again. And the threats from underworld characters. This is what I wanted to protect you from, Dan. Don't you understand?"

He reached out and touched her hair in a loving caress. "I

understand. It was a wonderfully unselfish thing for you to try to do, but maybe I can make you see things a bit differently than you have been—"

"Dan," she interrupted with a wail, "you can't quit politics. You love it. It's in your blood."

He smiled enigmatically. "I have no intention of quitting. Tell me, Lynn, are you a quitter?"

She looked at his beloved face and wasn't sure what to say. "I don't want to think so."

"Okay. When it happened, you were a kid. Younger than your years, really, because of the sheltered life you'd led. I can understand then why you'd run away. Later you had your mother to see to and she was ailing. So I can still see why you had to keep running. But now you're twenty-five and all grown up. I'm by your side and determined to remain there. Isn't it about time you stopped running?"

"But the threats . . . even on our lives. The scandal. It can destroy anything we try to build."

Dan made a funny face and shook his head. "No way. You telling me you're going to be a quitter? If that's what you want, I won't hold you against your will."

Lynn didn't know which of them moved first, but she was suddenly in his arms and it felt marvelous. His kisses were warm, sweet, and filled with all she'd ever need of passion and love.

"Ready to face the lions with me?" he asked when they had finally, reluctantly, drawn apart.

She nodded slowly.

"Then go put on some lipstick, for heaven's sake. Something seems to have happened to it."

"You're wearing it, senator," she retorted dryly, "and it really isn't the right shade for you."

She put on lipstick. He wiped off his. Hand in hand, they walked out of the hospital room, into the corridor crowded with security guards and curious people. Down they went in the elevator, accompanied by Dan's parents and several guards and agents.

Glancing over at her, he asked, right in front of all those people, "Are you prepared for the 'for better or for worse' bit? Let me warn you, there will be endless boring parties, dinners, teas, and charity functions. We'll have to spend days apart at times because of the nature of my duties. And I have a tendency to cheat at Scrabble."

Lynn looked over at him and thought her heart would burst with love. "I think I can handle that," she said softly, feeling more reticent than he obviously did among the other occupants of the elevator.

As soon as they walked out onto the top step of the hospital entrance, they were engulfed by reporters of every size, sex, shape, color, and disposition. Their questions flew out against the windy March air in an unintelligible garble.

Dan took hold of the first microphone that was thrust in front of him. "We'd like to make a statement. I'm feeling much stronger, but still have a period of recovery ahead of me. For that reason, my fiancée and I will make statements that I hope will give you enough information. If not, specific questions will have to wait until later."

Through it all, he held the microphone in one hand and kept her hand firmly encased in his other one. "First, I want you to meet Linda Marshall. I call her Lynn and probably always will. She is my fiancée and I hope she agrees to a rather prompt wedding. Show them your ring, dear."

Lynn obediently held out the hand which was graced with the lovely diamond Dan had removed from the chain around Herbie Bear's neck. He had lovingly, only half jestingly, promised the careworn bear a more suitably masculine piece of jewelry.

"What about the syndicate connections?" The ugly question came too frequently and too loudly to be ignored, even though Dan had stated they would answer no questions. Lynn had expected him to do the majority of the talking. Instead, he looked at her with a gleam in his eye and tightened the pressure on her hand.

With a strength she hadn't known she possessed, Lynn took the microphone from Dan and looked out at the crowd. "There are, my friends, no syndicate connections for Dan and me. I never knew anything of Davy Marshall's illegal activities. I still don't. Whatever is required of me to do to prove that, I'll consent, be it lie detector tests or otherwise. I was seventeen when this came down on me. My mother was not well and was scared, so we ran away rather than face it. My mother died, probably before she should have because of this. But I won't run anymore. Dan and I have talked it over and we're not going to be quitters. Later, when Dan's well, pump us all you want. You won't find anything illegal in our backgrounds."

"Aren't you afraid, though, Miss Marshall, that the fact that were part of an underworld family—even a totally innocent part—will hurt Senator Resnick politically?"

"I've worried about that, of course. That's why I ran away from him even though it broke my heart to do so . . ." Her voice trailed off and Dan came to her rescue

"If you don't mind, I'll answer that question. Then we're leaving. We have personal plans to make. When it is time for me to seek reelection as senator from my home state, I will do so. When the time is right, I will actively seek the presidential nomination of my party. Whatever occurs in the way of slander, prejudice, petty gossip, and suspicion, Lynn and I will fight. Being innocent as far as involvement in organized crime is concerned, that shouldn't be too difficult. We've nothing to hide. Lynn has suffered long for Davy Marshall's crimes. I won't be made to suffer. As a politician, I firmly believe I have a lot to offer this country. I'm not ready to call it quits. But I only have something to offer as long as Lynn is by my side. Without her, I'm not so sure I have anything to offer anyone. She's part of me and that is that."

Taking a firmer hold on her hand, he led her through the

cackling throng until they were safe inside the waiting limousine.

"You really think you have a chance of winning another election, Dan?" she asked fearfully.

He looked down at her and smiled. "Of course I'll win. When I want something, I don't give up. Don't you know that by now?"

Lynn smiled softly to herself, then let her head lean against his shoulder, her long dark hair spilling across the tweed jacket. With a finger, she traced the curling dark hairs around his gold watch.

"I guess I should know it. But, fair warning, you're probably stuck with me forever now."

"Make that a promise and I'll say I'll love you forever."

"It's a promise. For better or for worse."

He bent and kissed her fully, tenderly. "That's the 'better,' " he murmured. Looking out the windows of the limousine, he sighed in disgust to see the reporters still running along at its side. "And that's part of the 'worse,' " he commented.

"I can take it," Lynn said airily, locking her hands at the nape of his neck, letting her fingers tangle in his thick, black hair, "as long as I have plenty of the 'better' part." He met her eager lips, commanded them, and they both were soon oblivious to everything and everyone around them.